I0578293

# THE SWEETEST MATCH

## APPLEBOTTOM MATCHMAKER SOCIETY

### ABBY TYLER

# SUMMARY

When the owner of a tea shop discovers her shy, quiet cake decorator is leaving secret love messages in the frosting, the town solves the puzzle of who she is pining for and invents a celebration event with the sole goal of bringing the couple together.

Copyright © 2019 by Abby Tyler. All rights reserved.

No part of this book may be used or reproduced by any means, graphic, electronic, or mechanical, including photocopying, taping, and recording without written permission, except in the case of brief quotations embodied in critical articles and reviews.

This is a work of fiction. All the characters, organizations, and events portrayed in this novel are either products of the author's imagination or used fictitiously.

AbbyTyler
PO Box 160116
Austin, TX 78716
www.abbytyler.com

Paperback ISBN: 9781938150838

Edition 1.0

# MEETING MINUTES

## APPLEBOTTOM TOWN SQUARE PROPRIETORS
Gertrude Vogel, secretary
*Mainly because nobody else will do it.*

Today we met at the Applebottom Pie Shoppe, owned by yours truly.

We barely even got our coffee poured when Betty Johnson, owner of Tea for Two, which doesn't serve a single menu item that will power an old woman for more than five minutes, insisted we hear her first.

Her face was as pink as her jogging suit, which annoyingly matched the bows on her dog, which she takes everywhere, health violation or not. With her white hair all fluffed out around her widow's peak, she looked like the ghost of a valentine cookie. Except she could stand to eat a few. If she would put away a few slices of my brownie-bottom pie, we might could get some weight on her.

Nobody trusts a skinny cook.

Maude Lewis, co-owner of Applebottom Pie Shoppe, must have been thinking the same thing, as she got up and took a chocolate refrigerator pie from the cooler. She sliced it up for everybody and our Mayor T-bone (nobody knows his real name, and we're too scared to ask) about drooled on the tablecloth.

I took the largest piece and passed it to Betty, who tried to turn it down. But at least four hands shoved it closer to her, so she took a dainty bite like she was Scarlett O'Hara about to be laced into a corset.

Our civic duty done, we started getting chatty until Betty reminded us she had a pressing matter. She hired Sandy Miller a couple months back to decorate her cakes since her eyes weren't so good.

Even though we'd just served the finest pie you can get in the Missouri Tri-Lakes area, she brought out a container full of her fancy little petit fours.

It's not enough food for a bird, if you ask me, tiny little cakes barely an inch across. There's probably not enough calories in one of those tiny cakes to keep a roach alive.

Maude nudged me to pay attention. Betty was droning on about how intricate all the floral work was on the cakes. I was about to pop her fancy schmancy rose bud right in my mouth when Maude slapped my hand! Right in front of everybody!

Betty said I was missing the point and lined up all the cakes in a row. And that's when I saw it. Clear as a bell, the loopty loops turned into letters, which became a word.

*Handsome.*

I asked Betty who those cakes were for, and she said nobody special. Then she showed us pictures on her phone of an oblong torte with *maybe one day* hidden among the frosted leaves.

Another little round cake, if you skipped every other loop, read *regret.*

I said that girl probably did have a lot to regret, and Delilah told me to shut my nasty trap. Betty and Maude and the whole lot of them stared me down, so I did shut up, scrawling these here notes like I had nothing better to do.

Topher Smith-Cole of Applebottom Blossoms said it was romantic, and we should figure out who this handsome man was.

T-bone said Betty should watch the girl's eyes, as that would give her away if the man was still around.

Betty said Sandy never came out from the back, and everybody started talking at once, saying to make her come out and this was important and finally Betty said she'd have her do some work out front. That way she could watch her eyes, like T-bone suggested.

We agreed that we'd figure it out and come up with a good way to get them together. There was nothing like a good match of two locals to make a small town proud.

We ate our pie and the petit fours, too.
*Meeting adjourned.*

# CHAPTER 1

When Andrew McAllister walked in the door of Tea for Two, Sandy knew something had gone horribly, terribly wrong.

She got so startled by the unexpected arrival of her longtime crush that she fumbled her brush and accidentally stabbed the side of the wedding cake she was decorating.

She pulled the end out, frowning at the wound in the perfectly smooth frosting.

Why was Andrew here? She'd worked here for two months with no sign of him.

But the sly look on her boss's face told her the answer.

Betty knew. She'd seen the secret notes in the frosting and figured it out.

Oh, Sandy wished she hadn't done it.

Sandy kept her eyes cast down to the cake in front of

her as Andrew approached the counter. She couldn't look at him. She didn't dare.

What was she thinking, taking such a risk? First a few loops on a series of petit fours that spelled out the word *handsome*.

Then the words *if only* and *unrequited* hidden in the swirls of a wedding cake. It was going to Branson! No one there knew a thing.

But then there was *regret* entwined in the vines of Josefina's retirement cake. Surely nobody could have spotted them. They were half-covered in fondant flowers!

Still, he was here, and Betty looked like the cat who ate the canary.

That couldn't be good.

Her skin prickled as if Betty had cranked the heat. But of course she wouldn't have. School had just started, and the weather was still quite warm. In fact, Sandy could feel the gentle waft of cool air on the back of her neck.

Regardless, her body was on *fire*.

Betty got up gingerly from her stool behind the counter, a speed to be expected from a seventy-year-old woman who'd been sitting too long, even as spry as Betty was in general.

"Andrew McAllister," she crooned, and the tone of her voice set Sandy on edge all over again. Betty only talked like that to her poodle Clementine.

"Good afternoon, Mrs. Johnson," Andrew said.

Man, his voice was low and deep. The rumble in it made her belly quiver. Sandy hadn't heard him speak in months, not since he'd said a few words at the Applebottom High School graduation.

Thank goodness for the three tiers of the cake. She folded herself up as tightly as she could, squeezing her arms against her sides. She pretended to be incredibly focused on the tender petals of the peonies cascading down the back.

"Why, Andrew, you're a grown man," Betty said, her voice still high and squeaky, as if she were talking to a baby. "You can call me Betty."

Sandy rolled her eyes. This was too much. Betty never acted like this. What was her game? Would she show Andrew one of Sandy's secret tea cake messages?

Andrew spoke again. "With all due respect, I'm not sure I'll ever be ready to call you Betty. My mama taught me different."

"Such a good boy," Betty said, and Sandy stifled a groan. This was ridiculous.

Both Sandy and Andrew were in their thirties. Three years apart, in fact. They'd gone to high school together. Sandy had a terrible crush on him until her head got turned by the most foolish mistake she'd ever made in her life.

She felt a little faint. This could not be happening. Applebottom, Missouri, was way too small for something as juicy as this to go unnoticed. Probably the whole town was talking about the silly little words

Sandy Miller had snuck into the frosting since she'd taken the job decorating cakes at Betty's tea shop.

She could hear their voices.

*Poor little Sandy, all those years alone in that shack in the woods.*

*Sandy Miller is back just to cause a new scandal in Applebottom.*

*Now that her son is gone off to college, Sandy must not have anything to do but pine over old love affairs.*

Each voice had a face. And though she had spent the last eighteen years trying to silence the harshness of the words that had driven her to live in isolation while she raised her son, they were definitely coming back now.

Oh, that frosting. Why had she done it? Things had been going so well.

"Did you bring me that travel guide I asked for?" Betty asked.

Sandy peeked out from behind the cake.

Andrew set a large book on the glass counter. "I did. You planning to go to Spain?"

Sandy almost choked on the laugh that tried to come out. Betty despised airplanes. She'd told Sandy more than once that she'd fly high when she was headed straight for the Lord and not a moment before.

Betty must've heard something, though, because her sharp little eyes darted to the corner.

Suddenly, Betty's motivation to have Sandy decorate the cakes at a little table in the main shop instead of in the back became suspect. Betty had said it was because

Sandy's work was so popular that she wanted people to have the chance to watch it being created. Now Sandy wondered if this was her way of figuring out who the secret frosting notes were about.

She wanted to smack her own head.

Now it made sense. All the single men in Applebottom parading through the tea shop over the last few days. Each one having some strange little errand they were running for Betty.

Her boss was narrowing down the options.

She'd definitely seen the hidden words.

Betty tucked the book behind the counter. "I'll get this right back to you. What can I get for you, my dear?" Her eyes shifted to Sandy again.

Bingo. This was her plan. Sandy flashed back through all the other people who had walked in. Obviously, she hadn't shown enough interest in them, because Betty had kept them coming. All she had to do was keep her composure while Andrew was in the tea shop, and Betty would move on, none the wiser.

She took a deep breath, picked up her piping bag, and created a new cascade of pink petals to cover the hole where she'd stabbed the cake.

"I wouldn't mind a cup of your special Applebottom tea blend," Andrew said.

"Of course," Betty said, taking a mug off the rack.

"I should probably get it to go," Andrew said. "I'm getting my hair cut down at the barber shop."

"Nonsense," Betty said. "You're going to sit right

here and chat with me while you drink your tea. Arnold can wait."

Andrew laughed a little. "I'll let him know you said so."

"I'll ring him myself to let him know you are detained." Betty filled a mug with hot water from the machine and turned to drop in a tea ball with her special blend.

While they were occupied, Sandy leaned the opposite way so that she could get a better look at Andrew.

He wore a sports coat, even on a Saturday. He always dressed well, now as in high school. She'd always admired his wardrobe. He was more formal than other boys, and seemed more mature. That's what had intrigued her as a teen.

If only she had stayed true to those feelings then. But if she hadn't strayed, she wouldn't have Caden, and he was the joy of her life.

No, she couldn't wish for anything to be different. Not from her past. But this Andrew was here and now. He was single. He'd been Caden's history teacher for two of his high school years, though Sandy had taken pains to avoid being around him. Embarrassment, mostly. Or maybe she wanted to hold on to the old feelings without the risk of them getting ruined by reality.

Sandy had nurtured her crush on him, not having anyone else to feel something about, isolated in a small house on the outskirts of town with only a baby and her disapproving mother for company.

Those had been hard years.

But her mother was five years gone, and now, with Caden off to college, Sandy had ventured back to town. She had to. She needed a job and was relieved that Betty took one look at her paintings and agreed that she would make a splendid cake decorator.

And she had. Wedding cake orders were coming from as far as St. Louis now.

If only she hadn't started putting the messages in the frosting.

"Here you go," Betty said, handing the steaming mug to Andrew.

Sandy caught the mischievous gleam in Betty's eye as Betty turned her way. Oh, no, she was going to bring him over here.

Sandy set down the piping bag and picked up a brush. She didn't want to do anything critical while Andrew was so close. Her hands were already shaking.

"Did you know Sandy was decorating cakes for me now?" Betty asked.

Now that she heard the question, Sandy recalled the same line being said to many of the single male members of Applebottom in the last week.

This was a plot. How was she going to keep her cool with Andrew walking straight toward her?

She focused on her task with tunnel vision. Don't look up. Better to seem rude than to give the secret away.

She darkened the edges of all the pink petals,

making them more realistic. She tried to slow her breath and calm her trembling. Everything was fine. She could appear normal.

"I didn't see her back there," Andrew said. "I heard that she was working for you, though."

He had?

She risked a peek and found Andrew's kind blue eyes on her.

Her heart dissolved. All the emotions she'd held inside her chest for so many years rose up, magnified by his actual presence.

How different her life might've been. What might she have painted, lit from inside like she was right now?

"Hello, Sandy," Andrew said. "It's been a while."

"It has," she said, her cheeks heating up at the sound of her own voice, which warbled like a choir boy hitting puberty.

Betty's eyes flickered. She'd noticed.

*Keep calm. Stay cool.*

"The cake is lovely," Andrew said. "Do you do all this by hand?"

"I do," Sandy said, a hot bolt flashing through her that she'd just said marriage vows right in front of Andrew. A whole host of visions popped up, him in a suit and her in a white dress. Caden as the best man.

*No. Stop. Focus.*

Betty's eyes missed nothing. A small smile crept on her lips.

Sandy loved her boss. But right now, she really needed her to walk away.

Although it was quite possibly already too late.

"Why, before Sandy came along, I was lucky to sell one wedding cake a month," Betty said. "Now we're doing, what, Sandy? Five a week?"

Sandy nodded. She didn't trust her voice. She dipped her brush back in the diluted pink gel.

"Such attention to detail," Betty went on. "Did you know that a picture of one of Sandy's cakes was in the Branson newspaper society column? She was the talk of the city."

Sandy painted petals with the laser focus of cataract surgery. She couldn't give anything else away.

"Sandy was always an amazing artist," Andrew said. "I remember seeing her paintings in the school exhibits back in the day."

Sandy almost lost her grip on the brush. Really? He remembered her paintings?

She couldn't help but look up again. His eyes were still on her. He was so handsome, his dark hair falling over his brow, his strong jaw, his tall, lean build. She might be more attracted to him now than in high school.

She'd been a sophomore to his senior and shy as a wallflower. Andrew had been popular enough, but not athletic or bold. He'd been in the National Honor Society, a Student Council type. Well-dressed, well-spoken, kind.

Perhaps she'd been too young for him. Regardless, they'd never had a chance. Sandy's disaster had taken her well away from Andrew and high school. She never graduated or even got her GED. Pointless out in the woods with a baby on her hip and a town talking trash about her.

Shame coursed through her. She shouldn't even be looking at Andrew McAllister. He had three degrees. He'd been working his way up to becoming a professor when he'd returned to Applebottom. His father had died, and his mother was pretty poorly for a long time. She was fine now, but Andrew took a teaching position at the high school and stayed on. Sandy had known all this, even as isolated as she was out in the woods. Her mother still went into town and came back with the latest gossip.

"Well, I'll let you two kids catch up," Betty said. "I've got to mix the pimento cheese in the back."

She needed to do no such thing. The pimento had been mixed hours ago.

But Sandy found she couldn't fault the old woman as she looked back at Andrew, who watched her with an attention that warmed her cheeks again.

He'd never married. Sandy didn't know why. This was information the gossips didn't possess, although they had speculated all over the place. Maybe some college girl had broken his heart. Maybe he was too devoted to his mother. Sandy had paid it no mind. Only the truth mattered. She knew that better than anybody.

As Betty left the two of them alone, Sandy didn't care about the reason, only that he'd held off. Maybe, if she could be braver now than when she was a girl, the two of them could figure out a way to make up for the time they had lost.

If he wanted that.

His blue eyes said that maybe he did.

Perhaps she didn't regret the frosting after all.

# CHAPTER 2

Sandy Miller.

Andrew found himself tongue-tied to see her behind the cake in Betty's shop. And that was saying something. He always more than upheld his end of a conversation. That was why teaching suited him so well.

But not around Sandy. He couldn't put more than five words together.

He watched her paint pink petals on a wedding cake, astonished at how her artistry could transfer from a canvas to frosting. The flowers cascading down the side of the cake looked absolutely real. Resting on a few of them were tiny fairy sprites, mystical and lovely.

But even more beautiful was the woman herself. He found it hard not to stare.

The intervening years had not changed Sandy much. She was pretty in that small-town way that always conjured the idea of the girl next door. Her dark hair fell smoothly in a cascade to her shoulders. Her eyes were big and pale gray and full of wonder.

Back in high school, he'd thought they might actually work up the nerve to date. But then she'd been scooped up by Jerry Lavinski, a newcomer from a wealthy family. And everything fell apart.

Sandy got pregnant at just fifteen. Jerry insisted the baby wasn't his and slandered her far and wide. She and her mom had moved to a small house in the woods, and no one saw them much, especially Sandy.

But now she was back.

"How are you holding up now that Caden is gone to university?" he asked.

"Junior college," she said, and he liked that she kept things honest. There wasn't a bragging bone in her body. Never had been. "It's quiet."

"Is he doing well?"

Sandy nodded. "Football is his dream. He's living it."

"It's exciting. I don't remember the last time an Applebottom graduate has gone on to play college ball."

"I'm very proud of him."

Now that she was talking, his memory of her filled in its fuzzy edges. She was petite, now same as then, and dressed simply in a navy cotton dress with elbow-length sleeves. She never did take to fancy things.

"Your tea is probably steeped by now," she said.

"Oh!" He tried removing the metal tea ball, then realized he had no place to set it.

"I'll get you a saucer," she said, sliding her chair back.

She stood and hurried behind the counter, and his pulse increased. She moved quickly and nimbly, fetching a small white plate from a stack on the shelves.

When she turned, the skirt of her dress flared out just a little, and he suddenly pictured her at a high school dance, twirling to take his arm as they circled the gym floor.

As a teacher at the high school, he often chaperoned prom and the Harvest Dance, so these visions were easily kept fresh in his mind. But they hadn't felt so personal until now. He realized he'd never quite gotten over Sandy Miller after her abrupt departure from their high school.

She handed him the saucer, and for the briefest second their fingers brushed against each other. Andrew wasn't surprised at the electric zing that coursed through him. He remembered feeling it before, and marveled that it could have this much power through another eighteen years.

So much time lost since then.

Of course, he'd seen her now and then in the inter-vening years. He'd taught her son Caden twice. Sandy hadn't come to parent-teacher night, but she'd been at graduation.

"Did you go to Caden's football games?" he asked.

Sandy sat back down behind the cake. "I did," she said. "I like to sit up high so I can see the whole field."

And so no one would notice her, he'd bet. "I had him in class."

She picked up her brush again. "I'm sorry I never came to any meetings. He seemed to be doing well enough. I'm not one to interfere when it's not necessary."

Andrew found it hard to meet her eyes. She seemed chagrined that she hadn't been more involved with her son's schooling, but he couldn't blame her for turning her back on a town that had treated her so abominably when she had needed them most.

"Well," he said. "It sure is good to see you back around Applebottom." He gestured toward the cake. "I think you're going to be mighty popular."

She touched the brush to more petals. "I've been lucky. When that society column ran a picture, we started getting plenty of orders."

Her smile was shy and unassuming, and his heart tightened in his chest. He glanced quickly at her hands, pleased that there was no jewelry there. She had never married. What had she done all those years in the house in the woods? Did she still pine for Jerry Lavinski, the one that got away?

He dropped his tea ball on the saucer and sipped from his steaming mug. Arnold might be annoyed at his tardiness, but he was glad for an excuse not to leave quite yet.

"Can I take a closer look?" he asked.

"Of course," she said. "Betty has me decorate them

out here instead of in the back now. I've become a bit of a dog and pony show."

"It's remarkable."

She wiped her brush free of pink dye, then switched to green to add shadow detail to the dainty leaves beneath one of the fairies. "I can really only do one of these a day."

"I love how it's natural and magical at the same time," he said. He had the urge to reach out and touch it, but it was a cake, not a sculpture, so of course he couldn't do that.

"They're having a fairytale wedding. She's arriving in one of those Cinderella pumpkin carriages."

"Sounds fancy. You took art with Mrs. Hutchins, didn't you?"

"I loved her classes. I wish I could've done more." The last word cut off abruptly, as if she realized she was bringing up a sore point.

"The current art teacher at the high school is great," he said. "I hear she teaches a community class on Thursday nights."

"Does she?" Something sparked in Sandy at that, and Andrew smiled to himself that he was the one to bring that extra little bit of light in her eyes.

"You should think about it. This canvas isn't very permanent."

She laughed, and it was just about the best sound he'd heard in years.

"It's true. But I try to treat each cake as though it's

going to hang in the Metropolitan Museum of Art. That way I'm sure to do my best work, even though some two-year-old flower girl is probably going to stick her finger in it before the pictures."

Now it was his turn to laugh. He'd forgotten, or perhaps never even knew, that Sandy had a sense of humor.

Their eyes met over the cake, and it felt both as awkward, and as miraculous, as when they had locked gazes in their tender teen years.

He watched her a little longer, until all the green petals were painted, and she picked up a squeeze tube to put on more. His mug grew empty, and he had no more excuses.

"Well, I should let you get back to it." He set down the mug and had taken two backward steps, when he suddenly remembered where he was. "Oh, I need to pay for this."

Betty whizzed through the back kitchen door, almost as if she had been waiting.

"Oh, no, you don't," Betty said. "That was a thank-you for the book. You come back in a few days and fetch it, okay?"

She kissed his cheek. That woman was up to something.

But he didn't care. She'd brought Sandy back to him.

"Next time, I'll order some sandwiches, too," Andrew said. He took several more steps back, stopping abruptly when his backside hit the door. His face flushed.

"I hope you come back here real soon," Betty called with a wave.

Andrew reluctantly turned to the door. He might look like a bull in a china shop, his tall frame on those dainty chairs, but he'd definitely be back.

# CHAPTER 3

Betty still watched her.

Sandy lifted her frosting brush to add pinpricks of fairy glitter to the cake, but found her hand shaking so hard that her aim wasn't true.

"Now, wasn't that just the nicest visit," Betty said. "We adore Andrew around here."

Sandy nodded, not trusting her voice.

What did Betty think of that encounter? It definitely hadn't gone like the others.

Sandy's cheeks grew warm at the thought of it. Did she care if Betty knew? If the town did?

Sandy turned the cake carefully on its decorating wheel, suddenly remembering she had done it again, that morning, before she knew Betty's plan. Evidence, right there in front of her.

The words *second chance* were hidden in the swirls of the frosting, white on white. She took up a thicker brush, dabbed it in water, and carefully smoothed the letters out. There, gone.

"You really going to Spain?" she asked Betty.

"I might decide to travel in my old age," Betty said. "Especially now that I have such perfect help to watch over my shop."

Sandy didn't believe it for a minute, but she let it go.

"I didn't see Andrew much this summer," Betty said. "But he often travels while school is out. It helps him teach history when he goes to the places that he's talking about. I wonder if he longs for a companion."

*Aha.* Sandy kept her head down and added another layer of sparkle.

So Andrew was a traveler. Sandy hadn't been outside Applebottom since she was twelve years old. Her father had still been around then, and they had driven through the Ozarks down into Arkansas and stayed a couple nights in Eureka Springs, where there was a passion play at Easter. He'd taken off a year after that, leaving her to pick up the pieces with her brokenhearted mom.

Her father had not shown up at her mother's funeral five years ago. As far she knew, they'd still been married, but they had seen neither hide nor hair of him since he left. Maybe he was dead.

She was acutely aware that she was all the family Caden had. Well, at least all who would claim him. She thought for just the briefest moment about Jerry Lavinski and all his illustrious family. Not that it did them any good. Maybe one day Caden would take one of those fancy DNA tests and figure out his father for himself. She couldn't be faulted for his curiosity. She'd held up her end of the bargain.

Betty strolled up to the table. "My girl, I think this is the prettiest one yet. We need to make sure we get some pictures for the Insta-telegram feed."

"You mean Instagram," she said.

Betty waved the words away. "Whatever it is. Every time you post a cake, we get a dozen more people calling."

It was true. So was what she'd said to Andrew. These cakes had become everything to her since she'd taken the position with Betty. She was lucky.

This job was a fresh start for her. She could come back into town, visit with people, even though some of them might not be worth their salt. She knew what had been said about her eighteen years ago, when she turned up pregnant without so much as a driver's license to her name.

But she couldn't be bitter about it. Her cakes were popular, and her earnings were more than fair. On top of an hourly wage, Betty gave her a commission on each cake. She was doing just fine.

And now Andrew had materialized at their door.

Despite what he might've thought, she hadn't singled him out as the only teacher whose school meetings Sandy hadn't attended. While Caden was still around, she'd avoided talking to anyone who might make life harder for her son.

Caden was thriving and popular, and the last thing she wanted to do was upset that delicate balance. Caden had enough baggage to carry, no father, no grandparents, no real legacy. He had done all right, and she was mighty proud of him. If he was the only thing she ever achieved in this lifetime, it would be enough.

Except now she had this little slice of wonder of her own. She looked down at her cake. It truly was her best yet. What had Andrew called it? Both natural and magical.

When she looked at it, she felt all the promise for happiness that could be found in the world. Like weddings. Like family. Like love.

Betty had moved on, settling back on her stool. She probably listened to the whole conversation with Andrew.

Sandy checked the swirls on the frosting and chided herself for having been foolish enough to write the messages in the cakes. Now that Andrew himself was here, and given the sly look on Betty face, it wouldn't be a secret anymore.

In the years she'd had time to paint again, with Caden at school and after her mom was gone, she'd put plenty of hidden messages in her art. It expressed her longing, her dreams, and recently, her loneliness.

She never should have put any of it in the frosting.

But it had been so fun, sneaking those words into the decorations. She had been almost like her teen self, silly and secretive. She bet it was the torte that gave her away. One long line of swirls, and she just couldn't resist hiding a word. *Forever.*

Betty hummed to herself as she slathered sandwich filling on bread, more content than usual. Sandy watched her from the corner of her eye. Yes, her boss was definitely on to her.

It seemed like Sandy was destined to be the talk of the town all over again.

# CHAPTER 4

At school on Monday, Andrew struggled to focus. He was, after all, right there in the scene of all the moments when he'd known Sandy in their tender years.

He could point to the chair where she'd sat in his very room, back when he also occupied a desk, rather than the lectern. He remembered where she sat in the cafeteria with her girlfriends.

And the table where she'd moved during the brief time she'd hung out with Jerry Lavinksi's crowd.

He had to shake it off. He taught five history classes, plus a course in civics and government. This needed his attention.

During his lunch hour, a band of students arrived in his room to work on their debate team briefs. He'd formed the organization when he first returned, and this year he had a pair who might make it to nationals. They were devoted and well-spoken. He was proud.

The paternal feelings he had for them had been enough to compensate for his own situation. His mother needed him, since his sister seemed unwilling to visit the small town where she'd grown up. Her relationship with their mother had always been contentious, and without their father around to run interference, she'd only grown more distant.

Family was important to Andrew, and this was one reason Sandy's son Caden had stuck in his mind. Andrew had been right there when Sandy went crazy over Jerry Lavinski. But she'd never forced Jerry to take any sort of responsibility for what had happened. She'd removed herself from view, allowing Jerry to become the big man on campus, running through girls and, if rumor could be believed, some of the older women in town as well.

Even the teachers were charmed by him. But something was off, particularly whenever anyone spoke of Sandy. Perhaps Andrew had been too biased to see the reality of the situation. He always advised his debate team to be prepared to switch positions on any topic. You never knew which side of an issue you might be forced to defend.

He'd just never been able to see the other side of what Jerry Lavinski had done to Sandy.

During his off period, the school secretary popped into his room with an air of importance that set off his alarms. He knew that some of the ladies of Applebottom had something up their sleeve besides an unnecessary travel book delivered to Tea for Two.

"Sadie, what can I do for you?" he asked the woman, who was dressed in her usual colorful attire, a scarlet dress with a gold shawl and bright red flowers pinned in her hair.

She waltzed across the room in a swish of layered skirt, bringing with her a strong floral perfume. Andrew tried not to breathe too deeply as she plunked a sheet of paper in front of him on his desk.

"What's this?"

"Something right in the area of your expertise," Sadie said. She liked to wave her arms to express herself, and her dress had flouncy sleeves that made her look a bit like a flying squirrel.

He scanned the information on the page. "It's the one hundredth anniversary of the school?"

Sadie sighed dramatically. "As our history teacher, I thought you would have known. The historical date of our centennial will occur this November. We're having a great celebration in honor of this milestone."

This woman must have been an actress in her former life. Or maybe this one. He didn't know that much about her, other than her son ran the flower shop on Town Square. And that she was a hopeless gossip.

She did not need to work, having been left an impressive fortune by one of her late husbands. But she kept her position at the high school because it was the hub of all the best information on the town.

"I knew that Applebottom itself was over a hundred years old," he said. "And I knew the high school was built about sixty years ago."

"We were originally one unified school," Sadie said. "The original charter was signed in 1918, and as our illustrious man of history, we would like you to serve on the committee to plan a celebration in honor of our achievement."

Andrew knew when he was being strong-armed. "Okay. I'll do that. Do we have any other members, or do I need to round them up?"

"The first meeting is tomorrow," Sadie said. "I believe others have been recruited."

Andrew tilted his head at her. "So, if I'm in charge, who is putting people on the committee?"

Sadie waved her arms as if to brush aside his question. "Never you mind that," she said. "Just be at the first meeting." She tapped the page with her finger.

"All right. I'll be there."

As Sadie exited the room, Andrew read the contents of the paper more closely.

*Centennial celebration of Applebottom schools.*

*First committee meeting led by Andrew McAllister, Applebottom high school history teacher.*

*Tuesday evening at 6 o'clock. Main office conference room, Applebottom High School.*

He wondered who else had been invited, if that was

truly the case. Or possibly he'd be sitting in the conference room alone.

Somehow he found that unlikely. Sadie was too invested in something she normally wouldn't care one whit about.

He'd find out tomorrow.

Sandy reviewed her sketch of the cake, unsure of what she had done.

This one was unlike anything she had pictured herself doing. Not that being a cake decorator had ever been on her radar either. But certainly the creation in front of her was way beyond even her wildest imagination.

The entire surface would be black. Betty wouldn't even have enough black fondant to get the job done. Sandy would have to drive forty-five minutes to Branson and buy up literally all the black fondant in town to make this cake happen. But she would.

The theme to this birthday party was Gothic Punk.

Technically, it was a Sweet Sixteen party. The mother had shown up with her daughter, who definitely lived up to the style of her cake. The girl wore long black pants, backed by a skirt-like contraption that dragged on the floor behind her.

She had matching spiked wrist cuffs and a collar. At least ten ear studs lined one ear. The thing that had stood out, however, was the girl's golden blond hair. For some reason she hadn't dyed it to match.

Her mother seemed rather typical in yoga pants and a light jacket, her hair pulled back in a ponytail. She did assess both Sandy and Betty as the girl, who went by Fierce, put in the request for her cake. Betty excused herself, leaving the order to Sandy.

Sandy had carefully taken down each detail. Three tall sections, completely black, some silver flourishes. Black latticework. No use of the words *happy birthday* or *sweet*. Or *sixteen*. In fact, there would be no words at all, not even *Fierce*.

When Sandy asked for the location of the party so that they could deliver the cake, the mother informed her that it was a secret. "We are concerned with some of Fierce's classmates' juvenile behavior," she said. "All the guests of the party will be transported there by us."

"We have security," Fierce said with a hint of pride.

"Did you want to have someone pick up the cake?" Sandy asked. "It's going to be pretty heavy and elaborate to feed this many people. I'm just concerned that it may get damaged."

"I see," the mother said. She stared Sandy up and down for long seconds. Sandy must have passed some sort of test, because she said, "I tell you what, if you will be the person to personally deliver the cake, then I'm okay with that."

Sandy nodded. "That's fine. And you can tell me at the last minute, if it makes you more comfortable. As long as I can get there in time. It won't take more than thirty minutes to set up the cake."

"Very good," the mother said. She didn't even blink when the price was a sum that Sandy could never have paid for a cake. The amount of time to do the work, supplies, plus the delivery, made the order up there with a wedding.

Since her workload had otherwise been light that day, Sandy had decided to sketch it out and get a head start on some of the elaborate latticework that would be glued onto the cake once it was baked.

She had to paint the fondant darker than the original shade, because it appeared more dark gray than black. She knew Fierce wanted true black.

In the end, the cake would have a bit of a haunted-house appearance. That actually seemed sort of cool. It wasn't like Sandy had anything to compare this Sweet Sixteen party to, anyway. She had spent her own sixteenth birthday at the ob/gyn, checking on her third-trimester baby. And she hadn't received a single invitation to any parties after she dropped out of school.

But that was then. This was now. She wished she could have been more like Fierce.

Sandy had just packed up the last of her frosting brushes when Betty walked up behind her, holding out a sheet of paper.

Sandy looked at it curiously as she accepted it. This wasn't an order form.

"There's going to be a huge celebration for the one

hundredth anniversary of the Applebottom schools," Betty said. "They asked for a donation of a cake large enough to feed a couple hundred people. They thought it would be fun for you to create something that depicts the history of Applebottom with one of your lovely designs. The event is sure to be covered by the newspapers, and it's another opportunity to get your artistry in front of the masses."

The masses. In the Applebottom newspaper. *Right.*

Sandy had to hold back her laugh. "Okay, that's fine. When is the meeting?"

"Tomorrow. I appreciate you taking this on for me."

Sandy's eyes locked on a very familiar name printed on the paper. "Andrew McAllister is in charge of the committee?"

"Is he?" Betty asked, all innocent. She looked down at the page. "Look at that, he is. Is that a problem?"

"No," Sandy said. "It's just interesting timing, is all. Since he was just in here."

Betty retrieved her bag from a small locker and slid it over her shoulder. She clapped her hands two times, and her tiny poodle, Clementine, popped up from her little bed and jumped into Betty's arms.

"Him being here the other day is probably why he thought of us for a cake," she said. "Someone like Andrew would never stoop so low as to order something from the grocery store."

"I bet," Sandy muttered. Not that she was opposed to the idea. But it had just become even more clear that the town was intent on throwing the two of them together. She wanted to say to Betty: *Isn't it better if we get together on our own?* But, as always, she kept quiet.

Besides, maybe it was easier this way. They could figure out if they were compatible without the stress of an official date.

Who was she to question the ways of Applebottom?

# CHAPTER 5

ndrew tucked the last set of essays into a folder to take home. He had hoped to finish grading them all before the centennial meeting this evening, but he'd been slowed down trying to correct the grammar and spelling of a couple students who needed more help.

They'd also need extra credit if they were actually going to pass his class.

There were always the students who struggled. Andrew believed that helping them was more rewarding than anything else he did.

He locked his door and headed down the hall, his stomach growling. He should've brought a bite to eat before the meeting. And perhaps he should have thought to pick up a little something *for* the meeting. There was nothing worse than a bunch of grumpy committee members who really needed a snack.

Next time.

The halls were empty this late. He took the long way around, savoring the quiet. There was something about the school in the evening, after the din of the students had faded to silent. He didn't regret his choice to stay in Applebottom and become a schoolteacher. He'd let go of his dream of college professorship and tenure. Those opportunities might take him far from Applebottom, and his mother only had him to rely on. He would do the right thing.

The front office stood empty and forlorn. Sadie was long gone, as she often left before the final bell had even rung. The crazy teen drivers made her nervous, she always said.

Most of the offices were darkened and shut. The custodians had left a few lights on, however, including the ones inside the conference room.

He checked his watch. He was still about five minutes early.

When he entered the room, however, he realized someone had beat him inside.

He stopped dead in his tracks to see Sandy Miller seated in one of the oversized rolling chairs.

She was far less surprised to see him. Of course, his name had been on the flyer.

"Hello, Andrew," she said. "Looks like we're the early birds."

He set the binder he had prepared for the meeting

on the table. "Indeed, we are. Create anything crazy in the confectionery business today?"

"I did, actually," she said. "The not-sweet, not-pink, somewhat-undead sixteenth birthday party cake for a girl you may know. She's probably a student here. Goes by Fierce."

Andrew sat in a chair at the head of the table. Close enough to Sandy to talk, but not close enough to make people talk *about* them.

"I know Fierce," he said. "She has quite the strong personality."

"I'll say."

Sandy wore another simple dress, an indigo cotton number that darkened her gray eyes to the color of the evening sky at twilight.

Andrew's mouth went dry.

So this was why Sadie had acted so flouncy when she brought in the flyer. He bet she and Betty dreamed this up together.

"I have a funny feeling that we may be the only two people on this committee," he said.

Sandy glanced around the room. "It's not quite six yet." She bit her lip, and her mouth twisted in a funny endearing way that he suddenly recalled from when she was a teen.

"Sadie looked mighty pleased with herself when she told me about this committee," he said.

"Sadie? Is she still the school secretary?"

Andrew laughed. "She would never be cut off from her source of gossip."

"Is it weird to call her Sadie now? You refused to do it with Betty. Are there others still here from when we were students?"

"There are plenty of our old teachers still here. Did Caden not have any of them?"

Her eyes cast down. "Of course," she said. "He had Mrs. Bell, same as I did. And Mr. Winters still taught shop back then."

Andrew hated that he'd caused her embarrassment. He searched for a way to lighten the mood again. "You can't forget Mr. Fisher in the science lab."

Sandy smiled. "Does he still fall asleep in the middle of the experiments?"

Andrew leaned back in his chair, relieved to have moved them past a hard moment. "Now worse than ever. He always gets any student teachers that come through, mainly so they can supervise the Bunsen burners."

Sandy's smile expanded to a giggle. "It's so funny how some things never change."

"You sure haven't," he said.

She glanced down at the desk again. Dang it, he should've kept his cool.

But then she said, "You haven't changed all that much either. Still the best dresser in Applebottom."

Andrew tweaked his red bow tie. "With a new accessory sure to separate me from my students."

"I did notice that," she said. "Is that some sort of history teacher fashion I'm not aware of?" Her tone was playful, and Andrew couldn't help but smile at her.

"When I first started teaching, some of the teen girls tried to stay after school for extra help," he said. "I was quite uncomfortable with their attention, so I started dressing in ways that would lessen their interest. Now it's quite the source of teasing and notebook graffiti." The discussion made him self-conscious, so he untied the bow and slid it out from his collar.

"But I like it!" Sandy said. "It makes you seem so much more distinguished than the standard Apple-bottom citizen."

Andrew rolled the red tie around his fingers. "Well, you might be alone in that assessment. My own mother wishes I would leave it at home."

"You never told her why you did it?"

Andrew shook his head. "I wouldn't want her to be troubled. She has enough problems of her own."

Sandy folded her hands together on the table in front of her. "I heard about your father," she said. "I was very sorry to hear he had passed. I remember him fondly."

"Everybody does," Andrew said. "He was one of the people that made Applebottom truly great."

"I completely agree."

They looked at each other for a moment, a shared sadness between them.

"And your mom –" Andrew started.

Sandy shook her head. "Not the same." She stared at her hands, clasped so tightly now that her fingernails turned white. "She was a difficult woman. She made life hard."

Andrew resisted the urge to reach out and take her hand in his. He said the only thing that came to mind. "I'm so sorry." They were quiet a minute more, then Sandy looked up at the clock over the door.

"It's 6:10," she said. "Looks like it's just going to be us."

"I'm not surprised."

"You think it's a plot?" she asked.

"You figured that out, too?"

"I suspected."

Andrew's stomach chose that moment to growl loudly. He clapped his hand over his belly. "Busted," he said. "No dinner. Would you like to move this meeting to Annabelle's Cafe?"

She hesitated, and he wished he could take the question back. It would've been just fine for the two of them to sit there and talk.

He prepared to tell her never mind, they could stay at the high school, but then she said, "That should be okay. I just haven't been there in a very long time."

He realized that this might have been somewhere Jerry Lavinski had taken her. "Are you sure? I don't want to drag you places that have terrible memories for you."

"No, it's good," she said. "I've seen a lot of the townspeople in Betty's shop. It's time for me to be a part of the community again."

Andrew stood up. "Okay, then. Let's go give the town gossips something to discuss tomorrow."

He was rewarded with a full-throated laugh from Sandy. "You know, if I wasn't who I was, and you weren't the high school history teacher, I would be so tempted to walk into that diner and give them something to absolutely talk about for years to come."

"And what would we do?"

Sandy's expression was so unexpectedly saucy that he laughed out loud as well.

He was loving every minute of getting to know her again.

# CHAPTER 6

For Sandy, stepping into Annabelle's Café was like traveling through time.

Part of it was the decor. No one had seen that particular combination of mandarin orange and lime green since the 1970s. It had been dated even when Sandy was a teen.

The linoleum floor curled up at the edges. A row of cracked vinyl booths had seen better days. The tables and chairs that filled the rest of the room seemed on the wobbly side.

But the smells were as mouthwatering as ever. And as Sandy was ushered to a table in the corner, she felt certain the waitress had been serving there since Sandy was last here as a girl.

As she and Andrew sat across from each other in the booth, accepting menus from the white-haired waitress,

Sandy flashed with memories of this place from her youth.

Her eyes rested on a jukebox on the back wall. It still lit up like always, although it was quiet at the moment. There weren't a whole lot of people at Annabelle's at six-thirty on a Tuesday. It might get a little busier later. Or maybe it was dying out. Sandy had no idea how businesses outside of Town Square fared. In fact, until the cake decorating started booming, Sandy wasn't sure how Betty had kept Tea for Two open.

Andrew turned in his seat to follow her gaze. "You want to listen to something?"

"My daddy used to give me a quarter to play a song."

"Mine did, too," Andrew said.

Sandy wondered which loss was harder. For Andrew, his father was really gone. There would be no opportunity for reconciliation, new memories, forgiveness. For her, Daddy could be out there somewhere. Maybe he was dying. Maybe he was poor. She didn't see him as being someone successful and content. Happy people didn't abandon their kids and never look back.

She tried to pay attention to her menu, smiling to see that the food options hadn't changed in eighteen years. Pork steaks, grilled and sauced. Beans and ham hock on cornbread. Chicken and dumplings. Fried perch rolled in cornmeal.

Missouri classics. Plus a few burgers and chicken dishes thrown in for good measure.

When she glanced up, Andrew was watching her.

His blue eyes seemed to pierce this thick outer layer she'd built around herself during the years she'd been forced out of Applebottom. She could almost feel the pinprick of his interest needling its way inside her, like the first icy drop of winter rain after a long autumn.

It woke you up. And sitting across from Andrew, Sandy felt powerfully awake.

"What are you thinking about ordering?" he asked.

"The pork, of course," she said. "I haven't had a proper sauced pork since my mama quit cooking, about a year before she died. I never was any good at making it." She wondered if she shouldn't have said that. She didn't want Andrew to think she couldn't cook.

"My mom still does it," he said. "I've never even attempted it."

"Maybe she could teach me," Sandy said before she caught herself. It was the most presumptuous thing she'd ever said in her life, that Andrew might invite her home to see his mother. She amended it quickly. "I mean, send the recipe."

But Andrew didn't let her get away with it. "I'd love to have you over. Your mama didn't show you?"

"We didn't exactly get along."

"I'm sorry to hear that." His eyes softened. Everything about the way he looked and talked and behaved told her he was a kind man. But that made sense. He had been a kind teenager, too, when there weren't a whole lot of those around.

The waitress returned. "Are you two gonna keep

making googly eyes at each other or are you going to order?"

Andrew kept his eyes on Sandy. "Googly eyes, definitely."

The woman shoved her notepad back in her apron pocket.

"I was just kidding," Andrew said. "We're ready."

Sandy felt hot inside at the exchange. She knew she had been the one to be all brazen about how the town would view them getting dinner together. But faced with the reality of someone suggesting they were a couple, her bravado floundered.

Andrew's eyes swept across her, and he seemed to take note of her discomfort. He sat up straighter.

"Now, Flo, I know you remember Sandy. We're here on official school business. She and I got volunteered to head up the committee for the one hundredth anniversary. She's going to make one of her famous cakes."

Flo put her hand on her hip and sized Sandy up. "You used to come in here when you was a little girl," she said. "With your daddy."

"That was a long time ago," Sandy said.

"Time flies when you never leave this piddly town." Flo pulled the notepad back out of her canvas apron lined with pockets.

Sandy decided to cut to the chase. "Or when you've been banished for eighteen years."

Andrew turned to her in surprise. "He banished you?"

Even Flo was taken aback by Sandy's words.

"Bygones," Sandy said. "Skeletons best left buried."

"Amen to that," Flo said. But she regarded Sandy with something that looked suspiciously like admiration. "What can I get you?"

"We'll both have the pork," Sandy said.

"A woman who orders for her man. I like it." Flo snapped her notepad shut before either of them could argue with her. She seemed to have made her own conclusion. "And two iced teas. I'll bring them right out."

As she took off, Andrew shook his head. "Sometimes she brings me something completely different than what I ordered. Whatever she decides I need that day."

"I guess she knows her customers," Sandy said.

Flo hadn't taken their menus, so they set them together on the end of the table.

"You were right. We're going to make everyone start talking," Andrew said.

Sandy shrugged. It seemed inevitable. "I guess I prefer to be the one to start the rumors myself rather than have someone make them up on my behalf."

"You want to talk about those days?" Andrew asked. "Get it off your chest?"

Panic zipped through her. Did she want that? To air out her grievances with the town? Set the record straight about Jerry?

No. She wasn't ready for that.

"We're here on official business, so you said."

"I did," Andrew said. "So you think there's actually going to be a centennial? Or is like Betty's travel book, all for show?"

"I have no idea," Sandy said. "It does seem a little odd to have a one hundred year celebration for the school when really it's the town that's more important. But I suppose any excuse for a party."

"So what should we do for it?"

"Apparently, I'm making a cake," Sandy said.

"I'm on pins and needles waiting to see what you do."

"You think we can figure out some historical points for it?" she asked. "I don't even know what we have. The Missouri Compromise?"

Andrew choked on a laugh. "Yeah, we could really liven that party up over past sins."

So could Sandy. Her past was a littered with land mines.

"I guess it could be all pine trees, mountains and lakes."

Andrew sat back in the booth. "Now, I've only talked to you twice since your big return, but I think I already know you want to be a little more devious than landscapes."

"Oh, my dear co-conspirator, you have no idea what I can hide beneath little trees and swirl into mountain streams."

He lifted an eyebrow at that, and Sandy realized she already had some ideas.

# CHAPTER 7

Thursday proved slow, with no cake to decorate and the case full of petit fours, these without any secret messages.

Sandy sat at her designated table in the back corner of Tea for Two, idly sketching ideas for the centennial cake. Without even trying, she and Andrew had spurred quite a bit of talk about the two of them, having spent hours at Annabelle's Café working through their ideas.

Only when Annabelle herself came up to say that it was closing time had they realized exactly how many hours had passed.

And speaking of closing time, it was almost the hour for the tea shop to lock up. Betty had already put away most of the items that needed refrigeration overnight. Sandy felt a little suspicious of the woman, though, because she kept looking at the clock in a way she never did on an ordinary end of day. Sandy was tempted to ask Betty what she was waiting for, but something told her to let it lie.

She'd started packing up her own sketchpad and supplies when Betty said, "Sandy love, I'm going to let you close up. I have an appointment to make, and I'd rather we not shut down early."

Sandy glanced at the clock. It was only five minutes until the time they always locked the door. No one was in the shop. This seemed a little suspicious. But she only said, "I'd be happy to."

Betty headed to the back to collect Clementine. After a moment, she came back through with her dog and a wave. "Put away those last few lemon cake slices, if you don't mind!" she called as she walked out.

"Will do," Sandy said, still feeling suspicious.

She waited until precisely four o'clock, then slid the lemon cake out of the case to take to the back room. As she closed the refrigerator, the front doorbell jingled. Someone had come into the shop.

"Technically, we're closed, but I could get you some coffee or tea before I clear it out," she said as she entered the main room.

Then she stopped.

It was Andrew.

*Aha.*

"Betty asked me to drop by at closing time to collect my book," Andrew said. "She was quite adamant that I arrive specifically at this time."

Sandy laughed. "That's why she skedaddled out of here so quickly. She wanted to get us alone."

Now it was Andrew's turn to laugh. "They're really throwing us at each other, aren't they?"

"They are." Sandy walked to the windows to peer out. "I bet they're watching right now."

"It's fine. I don't particularly need the book right now," Andrew said.

"That's a good thing, because I don't see it anywhere."

Andrew shook his head. "Which means I'll have to come by yet another time to fetch it."

"And Betty will be so apologetic that she forgot that you were coming today."

"They've really got the number on us," Andrew said. "Since I'm here, can I help you with anything?"

Sandy headed to the door and switched the sign from open to closed. "Should I lock the door? Just seems salacious under the circumstances."

"I say give them a little more to talk about. We're two adults. Besides, what are we going to do in a tea shop?"

Sandy's cheeks grew hot, but she kept her thoughts to herself and twisted the lock.

"Did you come up with any sketches for the cake yet?" Andrew asked.

"I did. They're over here."

They headed to the back corner.

"Should I brew us some coffee since we're here?" Sandy asked.

Andrew glanced at the front of the shop, which was completely made of windows. A couple townspeople walked by, glancing in at them.

"Maybe we should take this to the back. I feel like we're being watched," he said.

Sandy surveyed the windows. "You know what, let's go down to the pie shop for coffee. I'm sure Gertrude and Maude would be more than happy to serve as chaperones. They keep their shop open for another hour."

"Good thinking," he said.

Sandy made one more walk-through to make sure everything was put away, then the two of them headed out onto the square.

The air was brisk. Fall had definitely arrived, and leaves skittered across the pavement as they left the tea shop behind.

The sidewalks were mostly quiet. They turned the corner to walk past the doggie bakery. Betty was inside, feeding Clementine a cookie while speaking with Delilah, the owner.

"So much for having an appointment," Sandy said. "She didn't even leave Town Square."

"I bet it wouldn't take three guesses to figure out who they're talking about," Andrew said.

Betty glanced up and spotted them through the windows. She didn't seem to care that she was busted and gave them a knowing smile.

Sandy clutched her sketchpad to her chest. "I feel like it's the 1850s and you're walking me without a chaperone along the downtown streets of Savannah or something."

"Applebottom can sure feel that way," Andrew said.

They passed the floral shop. Inside, Topher and Danny stood around a tall table, putting the finishing touches on an elaborate autumn arrangement filled with brown and orange leaves, twisted sticks in sparkling gold, and, inexplicably, a cluster of red feathers.

"I don't know where that's going, but it's bound to be some fancy place I'll never be invited to," Sandy said.

Andrew laughed. "Sometimes they make strange concoctions just to get people's attention in the shop window."

They turned another corner to arrive in front of Gertrude and Maude's pie shop. "Is Maude still giving Gertrude grief for spelling her shop with an extra *p* and *e*?" Sandy asked.

"That will be the never-ending controversy in Applebottom Town Square," Andrew said. "And if that's as controversial as we ever get, I'm definitely okay with that."

He pushed open the door to the pie shop.

Both Gertrude and Maude were inside, talking behind the glass case full of pies.

Maude saw them first, her dark eyes lighting up at the sight of them.

"Oh, my heavens, look who it is." She touched her hands to her short curly hair, black sprinkled with gray, as if Sandy and Andrew were suitors rather than customers. "Good Lord, Sandy, I haven't seen you since you were a girl."

"You haven't been down to Betty's tea shop then," Andrew said. "She's been there for two months."

Gertrude sniffed, tugging on her apron. "We're having a bit of a feud with Betty at the moment. Seems that she thinks her petit fours are more appropriate for Thanksgiving than our pies. Can you imagine! Tiny cakes rather than a pie!" She shook her head so violently that her helmet of perfectly sprayed gray hair shifted from side to side.

"According to this one," Maude said, pointing at Gertrude, "I'm not allowed to step foot inside Tea for Two until November twenty-fourth."

Andrew walked up to the counter. "Now ladies, is that any way to set an example for the fine people of Applebottom?"

Gertrude's face screwed up like she'd just eaten lemons. "Andrew McAllister, I have been running this pie shop and feuding with Betty Johnson since before you were born. Save your lectures for those kids at the high school."

She pointed a long, crooked finger at Andrew, but Sandy could see she didn't really mean it. Gertrude had always been a sourpuss, but in her heart of hearts, she loved this town and everybody in it. That included

Betty Johnson and her evil petit fours. Sandy had heard all about it from Betty since the feud began two weeks ago at one of the Town Square shop owner meetings.

"Well, I do hope you'll stop by and see me anyway," Sandy said to Maude. "I've been making the petit fours myself lately, and I can speak for their quality." Her eyes traveled along the baked goods inside the case. "But there sure is nothing like pie when you need something sweet."

"Oh, I like this girl," Gertrude said. "You have grown into a fine young woman."

Sandy found a lump had formed in her throat. It wasn't easy acting friendly and brave when inside she was still a scared fifteen-year-old girl being shamed by an entire town.

She seriously doubted that Gertrude, of all people, had been kind. But she would accept that things could change for both of them, and that maybe Gertrude saying she liked her was her best effort at an olive branch.

"Could I have a slice of that cherry pie and a cup of coffee?" Sandy asked.

"Make that two," Andrew said. "Sandy and I have official Applebottom business to discuss, since it seems some of our citizens have taken it upon themselves to make the two of us in charge of the centennial of the school."

Gertrude and Maude glanced at each other in a way that made it perfectly clear that they were absolutely part of the reason she and Andrew had been recruited for this task. Maude slid open the door of the case. "Since this is official Applebottom business, your pie and coffee are on the house."

"That's what I like to hear," Andrew said. "Given neither of us had a choice in the matter."

Gertrude rolled her eyes that Andrew would dare suggest that his civic duty was anything but a joy.

Sandy giggled. She couldn't help it. She had so forgotten what it was like to roam about town. Until Betty had forced her to work out in the open, she had managed to keep to herself.

Since this whole thing with Andrew, she'd talked to more people than she had ever planned. She'd even eaten at Annabelle's Café.

What would be next? Selling sodas at the school concession stand? Decorating for the Harvest Dance? Chit chat with the quilting women or the Applebottom beautification society?

Sandy knew she would never do any of that. Some of the things these people had said to her eighteen years ago would ring in her ears all her life. It was one thing to forgive, but quite another to completely forget. She wasn't sure she ever would.

Maude heated up their pie, added a scoop of ice cream to both and carried the two plates to the farthest corner of the pie shop. They would definitely get no privacy here, but then nothing untoward could be said about them, either.

Sometimes Sandy could hear them say, "Looks like Sandy Miller is looking to get knocked up again," and there was no stopping the emotions it brought, even if she was thirty-three now, with a kid in college to boot.

When they were seated, and the steaming cups of coffee resting next to their plates, Andrew said, "Show me the sketches."

Sandy swallowed a mouthful of pie before pulling out her sketchbook. She paused for a moment to savor it. There were no pies like Gertrude and Maude's.

"So here's the part we talked about at first," she said, pointing at the bottom tier of the cake.

She described the details. The Missouri Purchase. The establishment of Branson as a tourist attraction, leading more people to move there. The founders of Applebottom, and the famous pie it was named for.

Gertrude's voice carried over the shop. "Seems strange to make a cake for a town named after a pie."

Maude pulled Gertrude by the arm toward the back of the shop. "Hush your mouth, Gertie. Nobody wants to make a pie to feed two hundred people. Leave the young people to their work."

"I did it thirty years ago at the Applebottom Centennial," Gertrude muttered, but she followed Maude out of the room to the back.

"Looks like we have the place to ourselves," Andrew said.

"Good," Sandy said, shutting the notebook. "I just

realized I don't want them to see what some of the other tiers have on them."

Andrew grinned. "I definitely like the element of surprise."

They sat in companionable silence, eating their pie before the ice cream melted. Only when the plates were pushed aside did they take up conversation again.

"That's good pie," Sandy said. "I could come over here and eat it every day."

"I'm sure they'd love that," Andrew said. "Particularly in light of the feud they're having with Betty."

"I guess they just need drama to keep going."

"I imagine so. That sometimes happens to people who never leave their small town." Andrew sat back in his chair. He still had his bow tie on today, and Sandy smiled at seeing it.

"What about you?" she asked. "Seems like you were on the path to leaving Applebottom for good."

"I still probably will," he said. "But not for now. My degrees can wait. I'm needed here."

"Tell me what it was like to be at college."

Andrew stared down into his cup. "The words *college professor* sounded like just about the smartest, grandest thing I could do. I got to be a teaching assistant during my doctorate study. I actually had my own subset of students that I taught in a smaller setting." One of his fingers traced the rim of the cup. He didn't meet her eyes.

"I guess that's how you had the experience to come in and teach Applebottom's finest."

"It was. I didn't have a teacher certification when I got here, but it was easy to add to my degrees. And I'm not saying I regret it."

"But…"

"But I would eventually like to get back on my career path. I just don't know where that direction will take me." He looked up then, and Sandy's heart fluttered at the vulnerability in his expression. "So, for right now, I'll be content right here."

Sandy was glad for that, but she couldn't say it out loud. Not with Maude and Gertrude only a room away.

"What about you?" Andrew asked. "What were your dreams?"

"I'm not sure that I've had any dreams for long time. It was all about raising Caden."

"But now?"

Sandy gripped her mug. "I guess I would love to learn more art styles. I don't have any delusions that I'll ever actually do anything with my work. But if I had a dream, it would be to have something in the Metropolitan Museum of Art in New York City." She flashed him an easy smile. "Although it does seem that being dead a hundred years is helpful in that matter."

"What are you doing to get you there?"

"For dying plus one hundred years?"

He laughed. "No, for learning new styles."

"I still draw and paint. And now that you told me about the art class, maybe I'll do that."

"If your paintings are anything like your cakes, you'll succeed."

Sandy shook her head. "I don't think it's hard to overachieve on a cake. For real art, that's a whole different matter. I read some magazines. There's so much to it. Getting in galleries. It doesn't even have to be how good you are. There's millions of really good artists all over the world. It's who you know. I don't really want to aspire to something I can never have."

Andrew leaned forward. "Well, for the record, I believe you will absolutely see your work in the Metropolitan Museum of Art in New York City. I have faith."

Sandy mustered up her courage to look him in the eye. "That just seems ridiculous," she said.

"I think our biggest dreams always seem ridiculous. That's what makes them our biggest dreams."

She could see that he meant every word. Her chest loosened a little. This was the Andrew she remembered. Both practical and a dreamer.

Her life had been so lock-step for eighteen years. A mother to endure. A child to raise. Meals, clothes, school, schedules, homework.

Now her life was hers.

Maybe she could afford to dream a little.

# CHAPTER 8

*A*ndrew struggled all day Friday to focus on his students. It didn't help that his classes were in review, ramping up for when they would start new material.

On top of that, it was pep rally day, and the football team, which actually started to show some promise, had brought on a new era of school spirit.

Between the altered schedule and everything feeling off, Andrew decided to escape his room for lunch to commiserate with other teachers in the faculty lounge.

He shouldn't have been surprised to find the room empty. The abbreviated schedule often meant teachers were running around more than usual. He unpacked his turkey sandwich and stared out the window at the empty backfield. He was on good terms with most everybody on the faculty at Applebottom High School, but he wasn't sure he could call any of them actual friends.

Normally, this didn't matter. Most everything that concerned him involved the school itself, so he could easily speak with other teachers.

But this was an affair of the heart. It needed someone familiar with Applebottom, but who also understood the complexity of dating. Especially when trying to pursue someone you'd known your entire life and who had a difficult history.

Paul Hinkle, the math teacher, came through the room to heat up his microwave lunch. Andrew discounted him out of hand. Paul had been married for thirty-some-odd years. He doubted anything Paul could advise him on would be relevant to a modern situation.

They struck up a friendly light conversation about the annoyance of the pep rally day, then Paul took his lunch and left.

Two women came in next, elective teachers who covered Home Ec and technology. Both married. They talked quietly and kept to themselves.

The two of them hung out near the copier. As Andrew finished his sandwich, he decided he would just have to figure this out for himself.

But then the football coach, Carter McBride, walked in, heading straight for the refrigerator.

Carter had dated a lot since arriving two years ago. He had to know something.

Carter retreated from the depths of the refrigerator

holding a Tupperware container. As he heated it up, Andrew asked, "You going to eat that in here?"

"Sure," Carter said, peering inside the microwave. "Just give me a sec."

The other two women seemed engrossed in their own conversation, so Andrew figured it was safe enough to talk about Sandy. He folded up the wrapping from his sandwich and glanced at the clock. He still had a good fifteen minutes.

Carter sat down beside him. The intense odor of broccoli and cauliflower and other steamed vegetables overpowered what was left of the smell of Andrew's sandwich.

"Well, you know how to eat healthy," Andrew said.

Carter shoved his fork into the collection of vegetables.

"Comes with the territory. Can't ask the team to eat right if you're holding a corn dog." He stabbed a piece of broccoli. "So what's up? Rumor has it you've been hanging out with that girl who used to go to high school here."

Well, that was easy. "Yeah, but it's a little complicated."

Carter pointed at him with a forkful of zucchini. "How so? She likes you. You like her. Sounds pretty simple to me."

"Do you know what happened to her eighteen years ago?" Andrew asked.

"I heard she had a kid. Dropped out. What's that got

to do with you?" He paused, his eyebrow lifting. "You're not the secret baby daddy, are you?"

"No, no," Andrew said. He thought everyone knew it was Jerry Lavinski, but then Carter hadn't grown up here. "It was a guy we went to high school with."

"I thought he denied it. That there was more than one."

Andrew tensed up. Those rumors needed to die right now.

"They were wrong. Everybody in this town did wrong by her."

"Okay, okay," Carter said. "I believe you over the rumor mill, for sure."

"It's all started up again?"

"Just among the trouble makers. I don't take any stock in it. You do you, dude."

"You see why it's complicated then, though, right?"

"I guess. Were you friends with this Jerry guy?"

"No way."

Carter chewed thoughtfully. "And you're positive it was him? This town is sort of small for him to get away with something like that."

"She was really into him," Andrew said. "But it's not like I can ask her."

"Why not?"

"She moved out of town and avoided all of us for eighteen years over it. I doubt she wants me to bring it up."

"It's going to get in the way. I'd do it now before things get harder."

"What do you mean?"

"Just that secrets have a way of pushing people apart."

Andrew turned his water bottle around and around on the table. "I don't know how to approach her with it. Or when. I'm not sure how to ask her out, either. And if she says no, what do I do then? Let it rest?"

"I can help on that part," Carter said. "Go easy. Figure out something that she really wants to do, and give her the opportunity to do it with you. It's really as simple as that. If you know her, even a little bit, and it sounds like you know her a lot, you probably know what she likes. Start with that. Not like a date. But the two of you doing something you both want to do."

"Is that how it started for you and Ginny?" Andrew asked.

"Oh, no, the town forced me to help her with her dog."

"Betty and company are throwing us together at every opportunity," Andrew said.

Carter shoved the last scrape of vegetables in his mouth and swallowed quickly. "I gotta run. But let me tell you, this town seems to know things. I wouldn't have believed it before. But I believe it now."

"You really think so?"

Carter stood up. "I'd bet my team on it. They recognize something you don't know. So just go with it. Ask her to something. You only miss the shots you don't take."

When Carter left, Andrew took his time tossing his trash and heading back to his room. He couldn't stop thinking about what Carter had said. About the secret. And the date.

Keep it simple. Just ask her.

And find something that Sandy would already want to do, and do it with her.

But what puzzled him most of all was what Carter said about the town. What did they see that they weren't telling?

# CHAPTER 9

As Andrew walked the few blocks of Town Square toward Betty's tea shop, he practiced what he planned to say to Sandy over and over again.

What he would be asking her to do wasn't small. But he felt the need to go big on this. It seemed that everything they had done together since reconnecting had been related to the centennial event or some excuse the old ladies of Applebottom had put together to get them in the same room.

This one would just be all him. It was nerve-racking, truth be told. He hadn't asked a woman out in years.

Not that he *never* had. He'd dated some smart young women during his seven-year stint getting his doctorate in history.

Unfortunately, all of them had strong aspirations and ultimately left to pursue careers.

Andrew had loved his time at Mizzou, caught up in

the culture, the rigor of study, and the people he could talk to at great length about the subjects that interested him the most — history, art, philosophy, civilization, government. All the women he had dated met those criteria in spades, but he admitted that the romance side of things had taken a backseat to their intense conversations.

Perhaps that was the reason his heart never felt broken when they inevitably went to pursue tenure at some far-flung university or take sabbaticals to other countries.

On one of his trips two years ago, he'd even visited one, curious if he could rekindle anything they felt as undergraduates.

But nothing that happened changed either of their minds about their current paths. Andrew was committed to staying in Applebottom, seeing to his mother and helping the town grow from its rural roots into a more open-minded, civil community.

He tried not to be uppity or snooty or pretend that he knew more important things than they did. Applebottom had its own pursuits. Certainly no one could surpass Gertrude and Maude with the alchemy they used to create pies. And Delilah had turned a doggy bakery into something akin to a movement on behalf of all the animals, both domestic and wild, that lived in the Table Rock Lake area.

Even Arnold, with his barber shears and traditional candy-striped pole, made sure he was up-to-date on the latest hairstyles for men, no matter what the background, ethnicity, or hair type. And he didn't judge Fierce when she showed up wanting to shave one side of her head.

It was a good town, and a good place to live. His father had raised his family there. Andrew hadn't been held back in any way. And there was something about having a community when you needed it. His mother certainly had. The loss of his father had sent her into a spiral. Sadie had started a quilting circle for no other reason than to get his mother to join.

As he approached Betty's tea shop to ask Sandy to go on an excursion with him, he realized something important. When she quit Applebottom high school, pregnant and shunned, it had left a hole in him.

He'd cared about Sandy Miller from the start.

And today, hopefully, would be the first day that he would be able to take the opportunity to show it.

The door jingled. Betty looked up in surprise. "Andrew McAllister, what a joy to see you. I guess you came for your book?" She glanced over to the corner. Andrew had already spotted Sandy at her table, decorating a large rectangular cake.

"No, I forgot all about it."

"Good. Because I don't have it here." His answer seemed to please Betty intensely, and he sensed Sandy shifting in her chair in the corner. Now she knew he was there just for her.

He glanced up at the clock. "Time to make your pimento cheese spread again?" he asked.

Betty's eyebrows shot up. He'd called her out.

She stepped down from her tall stool. "I reckon I better get to it."

"I'll take one of those when you're done."

She tilted her white-topped head at him. "Now, Andrew, I've known you since you were knee-high to a grasshopper, and you've never once eaten one of my pimento cheese sandwiches. You take turkey on wheat."

"Maybe it's time to expand my horizons," he said.

"All right. Probably time to convert you anyway." She headed to the back, leaving him and Sandy alone.

Andrew approached the table. The cake appeared to be a battle of many brightly colored blobs.

"Good afternoon," he said. "What's this?"

Sandy turned a printed piece of paper around so that he could see it.

"A Pokémon battle," she said. "I wondered when I was going to get a cake order like this."

"I used to trade those cards."

"Everybody did. Apparently it's still a thing."

"Pokémon will never die."

"And not on my battlefield," she said. "I'm dropping in the body shapes right now so I can block it out."

"They couldn't get a licensed cake from some grocery store in Branson?"

"They could, and they should. But this mom likes to

support her local tea shop." Sandy shrugged. "I'll do it. It's something different."

She turned the page back around to face her. After studying it a moment, she picked up a palette of sorts, smearing some pink and brown frosting together to create a dull flesh tone.

"What's that one?" Andrew asked.

"Something called a Cleffa," Sandy said.

"There are so many. I could never keep track past a Squirtle and Charmander."

"I had to create a cheat sheet."

He watched with fascination as she swiftly filled a small bag and piped in a perfect shape, round on the bottom and pointed at the top. She picked up a dark brown bag of frosting and added a triangle to each side.

"Star-shaped," she said before he could ask.

"I don't think I would have the patience for this," he said.

"I like the details and the textures. I've learned a lot working here. It's not just frosting and fondant. I can make things with hard shells, or crunchy or glittery or paper thin. I've even gotten to work a little bit with gold leaf."

"You can eat that?"

"Oh, yes. You can get 24-karat edible leaf. I don't even want to think about the digestive process."

"You can put anything on a cake to make the art, I guess."

"Just about."

She'd provided him an opening. He opened his mouth to ask the question, but the words didn't come. He realized he was shuffling his feet and forced himself to stand still.

Finally, she looked up. "Did you have something you needed? Is everything okay with the committee?"

He needed to act. His courage was fleeing fast.

"I called over to the University of Missouri yesterday," he said in a rush. "This professor I used to know was still there. He's pretty famous for his mixed-media art. It just like what you're talking about. Textures and various techniques to make three-dimensional art."

Sandy paused with her bag of frosting, leaving the Pokémon with only one eye. Or maybe it only needed one eye. He didn't know.

"I know what mixed-media means," she said carefully.

He was botching this. Should he quit or keep trying?

He pressed on. "I've been meaning to go up there and visit, and I thought you might want to come. To see his work. The mixed-media, I mean. Since you were so interested in all the textures on your cakes. I thought it might help."

His words all ran together. He sounded like he was seventeen again. He hadn't gotten any smoother at this, despite earning three degrees and delivering thousands of lectures.

Sandy set down her frosting. "Are you asking me to

go to Columbia with you? That's a four-hour drive each way."

"It is far," he said. "I know you may be too busy to do something like that."

"When?"

"I was thinking about the holiday on Monday."

Sandy picked up the bag of frosting and added a second eye to the Pokémon. "Are you asking me for personal reasons or professional ones? For the centennial cake?"

He didn't know which one was the correct answer. His entire body felt on fire as he tried to figure out the right thing to say.

Then he remembered Carter's advice. Keep it simple.

"I thought it might be a fun outing for us."

At that, Clementine let out a single sharp bark in the back, and Betty shushed her.

The town was always listening.

Sandy glanced at the door. "I'm sure she's dying for my answer," she whispered.

Andrew leaned in. "We should totally mess with her by having a big argument."

Sandy giggled. "You're terrible."

She sat up straighter. "Andrew! You are much too forward! What will I ever do with my reputation after your outrageous overture?"

She almost dissolved into giggles again, but covered her mouth and held them in.

"I meant no offense, Lady Miller," Andrew announced. "Perhaps one of the fair dowagers of this shire will be willing to serve as chaperone to protect your virtue."

Sandy could barely get her words out over her laughter. "But you have a closed carriage!"

Now Andrew could barely get a sentence out. "I suppose I could rent a convertible."

And that was it. They both dissolved into laughter.

Betty came out from the back, holding her small white poodle. "All right you two. Fun's over. Sandy, you take the day off so you can make your little expedition to Columbia." She fixed her beady eyes on Andrew. "Without a chaperone."

She turned on her heel and stomped back to the kitchen.

"Sounds like the boss told you to go," he said.

"Is Monday okay for your friend?"

"I'll check with River," Andrew said.

"River? Do you mean River Montgomery?"

"Exactly. He also teaches in the art department at Mizzou."

Sandy pressed her hands to her cheeks. "I've seen all his work. But only in pictures. I can't even imagine what it's like to see them up close. A photograph doesn't do justice to mixed-media, not ever."

"Well, we're going to his house," he said. "Probably most of the things we'll see have never been in magazines. It's his private collection."

Sandy looked as though she might faint. "Yes, I'll go. Definitely."

Andrew stood up a little straighter. He'd done it. "I'll let you know what time works out Monday," he said.

Sandy's cheeks were still pink. "Okay. I can't wait."

And now, neither could he.

# CHAPTER 10

When Andrew rolled up to Sandy's house in a cherry-red open-topped convertible, she couldn't believe it.

She'd been watching from her window, not really wanting Andrew to come inside her sad little house. She didn't know why, but she didn't want Andrew to see how pitiful her life had been out in the woods all those years.

Especially not if he was going to pull up in a flashy sports car.

She had no complaints. The house was sturdy and strong. The roof only leaked in the kitchen. And it had sheltered Sandy and her son through more than just weather. It had been their home in their darkest days.

But it was nothing she was proud of.

Maybe one day she would have enough cake money to fix up the inside, give it a paint job and a real floor and toss the ancient furniture, half of which was propped up on stacks of magazines. But not yet.

Andrew killed the engine and stepped out of the car. It was so low to the ground, sleek and shiny, that he towered over it.

She snatched up her bag and hurried to step out the door.

"If you're trying to protect my virtue with an open-topped carriage," Sandy called, "I don't think this one is going to work!"

He approached her on her doorstep. "It's not my actual car. I rented it. I thought it might be sort of hilarious. And to be truthful, there might have been a small part of me that wanted to roll up to River Montgomery's house in something a little flashier than my Honda Accord."

She elbowed him with a laugh. "Is that your pride talking, Mr. McAllister, Applebottom's most lettered history teacher?"

"Guilty as charged."

Sandy turned to lock her door. "Well, I will guard your secret with my life."

Then she paused. "Is this like one of those historical novels where you need a wife with a title to make a good impression on your old school chum?"

"No, no," he said with a chuckle. "The car is as far as I'm taking it."

He extended his elbow, and she slid her arm through it. As a slow warmth spread through her body from where they touched, she realized she hadn't had this much fun in forever. In fact, she couldn't remember the last time.

Maybe there had been moments, playing on the floor with Caden when he was small, or when he said something funny or cute.

But certainly the optimism that flooded her in Andrew's presence was new.

It made her feel hopeful, like the world was opening wide.

Andrew opened the passenger door for her, and she slid onto the cool leather.

"It's so fancy," she said.

He circled the car to his side. "I know. It took me ten minutes to figure out how to turn on the radio."

Sandy buckled her seatbelt and smoothed down her simple black skirt. She had tried to walk the line between casual and dressy, not having any clue what sort of day they were in for.

Her sweater was simple, fuzzy with a bit of sparkle in the thread. Her only pair of earrings, tiny silver teardrops, gave her a finished feeling.

Andrew started the engine. "I can put the top up if you're worried about your hair," he said.

She touched it. She'd actually spent some time adding a bit of curl to the ends. It might be a tangled mess in the wind.

"However," Andrew added, "I did purchase a small gift for you in honor of the car. It might help."

He had done what? Sandy accepted the small flexible package wrapped in pale blue tissue paper. She opened it carefully, revealing a sheer scarf in watery pastels from blue to gray. As luck would have it, it closely matched the colors of her sweater.

"It's beautiful," she said. "Thank you."

"You don't have to wear it. I can put up the top. But if you would like the open top experience, this will keep your hair under control."

He rubbed his own head, ruffling his dark hair out of its smooth layers. "As for me, I will just have to suffer. I don't think I look good in scarves."

Sandy laughed. She unfolded the scarf and tied it around her head, tucking in the ends of her hair. "This is perfect. It's like I've become someone else for a day."

"It's a fun feeling, isn't it?" Andrew backed out of the gravel drive and onto the road. "But for the record, I like you just the way you are."

Sandy's heart stumbled in its rhythm. Everything was moving so fast. Caden's departure for college. Her new job and reintegration with her hometown. Committees. Newspaper articles. Now, Andrew.

She gripped the door handle as even the car seemed to whiz way beyond her ability to process the speed they were going. She knew Andrew was not the sort to drive above the speed limit, but it still felt as though she were hurtling toward a future she couldn't quite yet imagine.

The roar of the wind as they drove along the

highway made it difficult to talk. Even the radio was lost. But Sandy found the silence companionable and easy.

They drove almost three hours straight through to Jefferson City before stopping to take a break for lunch.

"I forget how pretty this drive is," Andrew said. "I think I might be over the whole open-top convertible experience, though."

"I agree," Sandy said, touching her lips, dried out after the long ride in the wind. "Although we should still pause a few blocks away to put it down again as we ride up. Just to be cool."

"Now that's an idea."

They entered a small café just off the interstate, part of a combination gas station and tourist shop.

"All you need to finish out your outfit and look like a movie star is a pair of sunglasses," Andrew said as they wandered the shop while waiting for the waitress to clear a table.

Sandy picked up a pair from a rack. "How about this?"

"Go bigger," Andrew said. He lifted another pair from its slot. "Try these."

Sandy slid them on and handed the first pair to Andrew to put back on the rack. They did these motions fluidly, as if they knew each other well, and made excursions like this all the time.

She turned to a mirror.

Goodness, she did look like a movie star. With the

scarf and the earrings and the sweater and the shades, she could put on an entire new personality.

"I look like someone who deserves to go to a private museum with one of the state's most renowned artists," she said. She twirled her hand in the air as though she were gesturing to her fandom.

"I take back what I said earlier. I love this version of you," Andrew said. "Let's get these."

They walked over to the register, but Sandy didn't allow him to pay for the sunglasses. She already felt a little overwhelmed with his spontaneous gift. Thankfully, they weren't expensive.

When they were done, the waitress spotted them and waved them back over to the restaurant side of the building.

As they slid into their seats, Sandy said, "It might be nice to have a conversation without an entire town listening in."

"They probably slipped a bug into our clothing at some point," Andrew said. "I was talking to Carter the other day, and he said that the town threw him and his girlfriend together, too."

"You mean the football coach?" Sandy asked.

"Yeah, Carter McBride."

"They are sort of meddling, aren't they?" She cast her eyes to the menu.

"I'm not complaining," he said.

Warmth coursed through her again. The words on

the menu blurred, and Sandy had to focus hard to make them penetrate.

"Pretty standard stuff on the menu," Andrew said. "I know a ton of cool little places in Columbia, of course, but I didn't think we could make it that far without eating."

"You called it correctly," Sandy said. "I was starving."

They gave the orders, and Sandy carefully untied the scarf and set it aside for the meal.

"I really do love this," she said. "You didn't have to."

"I wanted to." He opened his mouth as if he might say more, then took a sip of water instead.

Was he nervous, too?

"I'm very excited to meet River Montgomery," she said. "I hope I look all right."

"You're perfect," Andrew said. "I bet you went online and searched for every little thing you could read about him over the weekend."

Sandy smiled. "Busted. I couldn't go over to his house and look at his art without knowing all the important things."

"It's smart," Andrew said. "I do the same thing. When I was in graduate school, I got the opportunity to attend a private reception following a lecture by one of my most revered historians. I was so anxious about it that I actually studied nothing but his opinions for a full week, neglecting my actual graduate work." He tapped the table. "Totally worth it. He was very impressed by how up-to-date I was on all the important matters of government and history. From his view, of course."

As Andrew spoke about some of his exploits in his years at the University of Missouri, Sandy felt her excitement start to shift into mild dismay. How could she even hold a conversation with these people who had doctorates?

She had never finished high school. Not even close. She'd quit as a sophomore. She didn't complete even a second year of history. She knew nothing about politics. She hadn't read any important books. Her literature classes cut off at Romeo and Juliet. A five-year-old could repeat that plot.

Was she about to make a fool of herself?

She had read up on River Montgomery, but if he wanted to speak broadly about art, she would know nothing. As her stomach trembled, Sandy wasn't sure she would be able to eat a bite. And as for talking? It might be best if she just kept her mouth shut.

"I've gone on too long," Andrew said. "There's nothing worse than a history professor who doesn't know when to stop."

Sandy didn't have a clever reply to that, not even to counter his concern.

Luckily, the food arrived. Andrew lifted a buttered biscuit. "For a long time, I really thought that all of Missouri was the same," Andrew said. "But after traveling the state a good bit, I realized the regional influences are very strong."

Sandy could only nod. She hadn't been all over Missouri. She had scarcely been anywhere. She should never have left her shack. Or maybe, once she left it, she should have gone someplace new entirely.

Andrew expression shifted to concern. "Is everything okay?"

Sandy managed to avoid answering by shoveling a mouthful of pasta straight into her mouth. She shrugged her shoulders as if to say *I'm okay.*

Andrew let her off the hook, but certainly the easy camaraderie they had felt earlier had dissolved with Sandy's distress. She didn't know how to turn it around. She had so little experience in any of these things.

They finished their meal, and Andrew promptly paid. "We should get back on the road. We're expected at two o'clock."

With the top up, conversation should have happened, but the air between them was stilted. Sandy wished she were some other person, someone who had more in common with Andrew. If only she could say something smart.

But she was who she was. A small-town girl who'd paid the price for falling for a local boy who had no intention of sticking by her.

The silence lengthened, and her discomfort grew. This had been a terrible idea. She wanted to jump from the car.

But Andrew noticed. "Hey, you okay?"

"I'm fine," she said.

He tapped the steering wheel, and she wondered if he'd just turn on the radio to spare them any more awkward silence.

But he didn't give up.

"Any news from Caden?" he asked.

"Sure, he's good."

"They had their first game on Saturday, right? Did you go?"

The idea that Andrew had looked up her son's community college football team quelled a few of her doubts. He was trying so hard. Her chest relaxed. At least he'd found something they could talk about.

"Caden told me to wait for the first home game because it will be more fun. Plus the first two are so far away. He sent me a shirt to wear!"

"That will be exciting. Do you talk to him much?"

"He called me after the game. He played for three minutes, which isn't bad for a freshman," she said. "Apparently there was the funniest play. The quarterback fumbled after the snap and Caden jumped right in the fray to recover it."

"Did he get it?"

"He did! He emerged from this pile of football players all triumphant! I think every photographer in the stadium took a shot of it. A video clip of him has gone viral."

"That's excellent. Does he still consult with Coach McBride?"

"He called him after the game at something like

midnight," Sandy said. "I told him that wasn't wise, but apparently they had a great conversation."

"Coach is one of the good ones," Andrew said. "He really cares about his kids."

"Do you like teaching?"

"Love it," he said. "Mostly."

"Mostly?"

"It just would be nice to have someone to talk to about more than the dates and battles of the Civil War. As much as I try to get these kids beyond the text, they're really focused on testing and grades. It isn't quite the same as two people engaging in a conversation just to flesh out their feelings about some historical event."

Sandy understood that. "When I first started decorating for Betty, I think I drove her crazy talking nonstop about frosting brushes and piping tips and the texture of buttercream. It's so technical, and honestly the average person doesn't even need to think about these things."

"Exactly," Andrew said.

Sandy wasn't sure that she knew enough to talk about anything that interested Andrew, but she could try. "So, what was one of your most debated topics among your history friends?"

"Oh, there were so many. Like, how is it possible to document even the most objective of historical events when we all see everything through the filter of our own experiences and prejudices?"

Sandy turned to the landscape whizzing outside her window, her throat tight. "Most of my life has been a source of speculation and guesswork, pretending to be facts. But nobody ever asked me."

Andrew got quiet, and Sandy wondered if she'd killed their day right there.

# CHAPTER 11

As Sandy brought up the difficult subject of her past, Andrew gripped the steering wheel. He'd known this topic would come up eventually, just not necessarily on their first real outing together.

His mind scrambled for a response. He couldn't just sit there silently driving like an idiot.

Finally, he said, "I think most people in Applebottom today would agree that things weren't handled well eighteen years ago."

Sandy made a noise that sounded remarkably like a snort. "You know, it's taken me eighteen years plus the two months of working back in Applebottom to feel brave enough to even think about countering all the things that were said about me when I was too young and too scared to defend myself."

"That's fair," Andrew said. "I wish I had done more than I did at the time."

"You were a teenager," Sandy said. "And I'm sure you had nothing to do with those crowing boys who had so much to say when there was so little they actually knew."

"Jerry was at the center of all of it," Andrew said. He supposed that if they were going to talk about this, they might as well get this big issue out of the way.

"Of course he was," Sandy said, her voice bitter. But even as they discussed these difficult things, Andrew found he could not ask her straight out if Jerry was the father of the baby.

"I wasn't friends with Jerry or his crowd," Andrew said.

"And I'm grateful for that," Sandy said.

"I don't think it matters how large or small a community is," Andrew said. "There always seems to be jerks and liars."

"It's almost as though every town has a quota to fill," Sandy said. "I guess I was the token pathetic girl who didn't know any better."

"I never thought that," Andrew said.

"You were the only one, then."

"I like to think that we all learned something from what happened."

Sandy twisted the scarf around her wrist in agitation. "I don't think so. I feel quite certain that if some poor girl at the high school—Fierce, maybe—turned up pregnant, and the guy she thought she was dating insisted that no, this girl was sleeping with everybody under the sun, that the town would handle it no better now than they did eighteen years ago."

She was probably right. It was quite possible that Betty and Gertrude and Maude and all the old guard of Applebottom were only being nice to Sandy now because she had weathered the storm. She'd become a mother and raised her child in Applebottom He'd turned out great, and she'd come back to town. If the whole mess were to start all over again, it seemed pretty likely that the new girl in trouble would not be treated any better.

"For what it's worth, Caden is a great kid, and I'm glad he's around."

"That's not even on the table," Sandy said. "Of course I'm glad I had him. I just don't bear any delusions that the town learned anything from what happened to me."

They approached the outskirts of Columbia. The conversation had been difficult, so Andrew didn't feel the same sense of nostalgia that he usually did as he approached the city where he'd lived for seven years.

But as they returned to their quiet contemplation and more and more familiar places rolled by, Andrew managed to find a measure of peace in seeing the old sights. After suppressing several comments about places he used to go, and things he used to do, he decided that maybe it would be better if he did say them. Give them something new to talk about.

"I used to live in the neighborhood over there," he said, pointing out the window. "In grad school, I rented a house just a few streets off the interstate. I had two roommates, guys I thought I knew pretty well, but they turned out to be literally the worst housemates I could've ever chosen."

Sandy took the bait. "What made them so horrible?"

"Well, let's just say they liked the ladies."

"Was there an endless parade?" Sandy asked.

"To put it mildly."

"What about you? Did you date a lot during those years?"

Now that was a loaded question if Andrew had ever heard one. "There were a few here and there. But we all ended up going our separate ways."

*And. Stop.*

There was no reason to belabor any of these points.

"Do you plan to always live in Applebottom?"

He shrugged. "If I could convince my sister to come around a little bit more, I wouldn't feel so compelled to stay. But right now I do." He glanced over at her. "What about you? You don't have anything keeping you there."

"I don't know where else I would go. Applebottom is all I know. I could sell the house, but I don't think I would get much for it, not in its current condition. Maybe if I get enough popularity as a cake decorator, I could go to a city and get a job doing it there. But I feel like my earnings go a lot further here than it might in some place like Branson or St. Louis."

"You're smart to think that way," Andrew said.

"Do you miss living in a city like this?" She peered out the window at the houses as they passed. They were in the historic district, most of the century-old houses restored to their former glory.

"All the time. But when I was here, I missed things from there. I figure being content is not about pining for someplace else, but being happy where you are."

Sandy stared out the window. He'd forgotten that she hadn't traveled much. He should be showing her more. "Would you like to see campus? It's a nice one."

"Oh, can we? And I would really love to see some tall buildings. I've never seen anything with more than three stories."

He chuckled. "I think we can manage that."

He turned up Providence Road, passing shops and buildings and finally heading into the trees that surrounded campus. He always loved how natural the area felt, as if the University were nestled in its own green space.

He'd spent a lot of afternoons walking in the Grindstone Nature Area, contemplating his studies in history and philosophy. Those had been good years.

The thought of taking Sandy to some of these places made him smile. It felt right.

"It's so green here," Sandy said. Her nose was practically pressed to the glass.

"It was one of my favorite things about Mizzou," Andrew said. "Look up, we're about to go beneath the pedestrian bridge."

Looming ahead was the big brick and metal bridge bearing the huge symbol of the Mizzou Tiger.

Sandy held onto the dash and stared at it until they passed beneath.

"There's the stadium," he said. "Faurot Field."

"I love how it's called *The Zou*," she said with a laugh.

"I'm pretty sure the main building is the tallest one on campus," he said. "Let me see how close we can get."

"Oh, that's not necessary," she said. "Everything is so big!"

"You'll want to see it. It's the heart of campus."

They drove past red brick buildings and parking lots. He pointed out the dorm where he had lived as a freshman. They both puzzled over some construction, trying to figure out what might be coming.

"It feels so exciting," Sandy said. "And there's so many people. They're walking everywhere."

When they arrived at the center of campus, Andrew spotted a fifteen-minute loading zone spot and slid into it.

"We can't stop here for long or we might get towed," he said. "But we can get out for a second."

Sandy already had the door open. She stepped out of the car, the wind whipping her hair. She ducked back in for her scarf and smiled at him before retreating again.

She was happy. He got out and walked around to stand beside her.

Her eyes were wide and dove-gray as she took in the

brick entrance to Traditions Plaza, the black and gold flags flying behind.

"It's so beautiful," she breathed.

Jesse Hall rose just ahead, its clean, white architectural lines, red brick, and the gorgeous white dome reaching up into the blue sky.

"So this is what it feels like to stand on a college campus," Sandy said.

Andrew realized how much he'd taken for granted. "You could still go," he said. "Just get your GED. I can help you study if you want."

"I can't even imagine a future like that." She had tears in her eyes. "All the futures I never could have seen. But now I'm looking at one of them." Her voice was full of reverence.

It felt completely natural to take her hand, small and cool in the outdoors.

She squeezed his fingers and turned to him, wonder all over her face. "I feel like I could do anything while I'm standing here."

"It's the sort of feeling you can build on. Just take it in."

They approached the building, and Sandy took her time absorbing every detail. They walked along the bright white sidewalks and climbed the steps.

He led them around the scenic part of central campus for as long as he dared, but then they were risking being late to meet his friend. "You ready to see some art?"

Sandy couldn't take her eyes from the view around her. "I don't think anything is going to beat this."

Andrew had to disagree. "I think we've just gotten started."

# CHAPTER 12

Sandy could barely contain her nerves as they pulled up to the impressive two-story house with a huge porch. It had columns and gables, like a grand plantation house.

Sandy had never even seen anything like it, much less gone inside. She tugged nervously at her skirt. She pictured a butler and house staff and immaculately dressed guests.

They had parked in a circle drive, the car top-down, as they had discussed. But Sandy discovered that as they approached the door, she couldn't bear to leave on the scarf and sunglasses. It wasn't her. She shoved the sunglasses in her purse and tugged the scarf from her head.

Other women certainly could have made some clever tie around their neck, but she simply attached the scarf to the handle of her bag. She was so not up for this. She felt outclassed in every way.

"Don't be nervous," Andrew said. "River is a super funny and laid-back guy. He's also quite possibly shorter than you."

Really? The magazine articles had never mentioned that.

Andrew pressed the bell, which pealed the tones of the Hallelujah chorus.

A chorus of barking penetrated the door. Sandy and Andrew glanced at each other, wondering what pack of mutts they were about to encounter. It sounded like a hundred.

"Hush, babies, hush!" came a voice from the other side. The barking ceased.

"Well-trained, at least," Andrew said.

The door opened. Sandy recognized River instantly. He was iconic in art circles, wiry and eccentric, wearing a long dark purple waistcoat, a tuxedo shirt with a sunny yellow cummerbund, and shiny black pants.

"Andrew!" River said, his accent thick with deep southern twang, almost as if he faked it. "You made it!" At his feet, six dogs of varying shapes and sizes sat obediently in a cluster.

"You must be Sandy," he said. He reached out and took one of her hands to clasp between his. "Andrew told me all about your brilliant cakes."

He let go of her and looked down at the dogs. "This is MiMi, Lolo, JuJu, NayNay, Tutu, and Killer."

Killer looked up at the mention of his name. He was a tiny brown Chihuahua with a pink nose.

"Killer?" Andrew asked.

"He's a rescue pup. He won't answer to anything else." River waved them inside.

They all entered a large gleaming foyer with a set of curving stairs that led to a second floor.

Sandy drew in a breath. Everywhere she looked, there was art. All up the wall along the staircase. Filling every corner. Statues. Paintings. Installations of dramatic scenes covered the floor. At her feet stood a battlefield of dolls. Just beyond it, broken-up parts of a bicycle were strategically scattered.

"It's a lot to absorb," River said. "Take your time."

Sandy had never seen any of these pieces. "Are these yours?"

"Oh, goodness no," he said. "I buy from every starving artist I see. Most everyone has talent. There are very few hacks in the art world, and most of *them* fill the New York galleries." He laughed at his joke. "But isn't it all so perfectly wonderful?" He gestured at the room.

A walkway had been fashioned with short brass poles holding red velvet ropes a couple feet from the ground.

Sandy bent down to examine it all more closely. She was particularly interested in the shattered bicycle. The spread of the pieces spoke to her, as if suddenly, everything had fallen apart at once. This had been exactly what it felt like for her — a wheel here, a handlebar there, and no center to hold anything together.

"I love that one," River said. "I almost hate her for her talent. It evokes everything, doesn't it?"

"It does," Sandy said. She felt the urge to whisper, even though they were in a private home. Something about being surrounded by this much art inspired her reverence.

River leaned close to Andrew. "Don't let this one get away."

Sandy forced herself not to look over as he said it, although she could feel her cheeks heating up, undoubtedly staining bright pink.

When they reached a door at the far side of the foyer, River pushed through. "I prepared a light snack," he said.

They reached a sunny atrium at the back of the house, the entire wall filled with windows, and a skylight opening above. Every corner glowed with sunshine.

Sandy looked up at the glass over her head. "I bet that is amazing when it rains."

"I haven't come here during a rainfall in a long time," River said. "Andrew, leave this diamond to me. I think I need her for inspiration."

"Not a chance," Andrew said.

A glow spread through Sandy's belly. This afternoon could not have been more different than almost every day that had come before it. She'd been so isolated and alone. Going about her days with no one who understood what made her heart sing. And now, here she was, surrounded by the most impossible things and being told how special she was.

She wondered if she had died somehow, and this was her afterlife. Nothing felt real.

At the far end of the atrium sat a large glass-topped wicker table with six chairs. Three place settings had been prepared, and as they approached, Sandy spotted several bowls of fruit, a small tray of sandwiches, and a basket of cakes.

Sandy peered into it, then gasped at the petit fours inside. "Those are mine," she said.

"They are, my girl," River said. "When Andrew refused to stop filling my ear with talk of you, I immediately rang up your little tea shop and ordered a set of cakes so that I could take a peek."

Did he know about the secret messages? These were fairly fresh, so they were a newer batch that didn't have them anymore. Did Andrew know? He'd never brought the messages up. Hopefully Betty had been discreet enough not to mention them directly to him, but if half the town knew…good Lord. Why had she done it?

She sank into a seat, and River poured tea into each of their cups. "So tell me, Sandy, whatever prompted you to take up cake decorating?"

Sandy's mouth went dry. She didn't want to explain how she needed a job because she was about to lose her house, even as sad and rundown as it was.

Her brain whirred, trying to come up with an answer, but River had mercy on her and breezed on.

"Never mind that. Jobs are boring." He picked up one of the petit fours decorated with the minuscule head of Betty's white poodle Clementine, complete with pink bows over her ears.

"I have never seen such a perfect rendering of a puppy dog in frosting," River said. "One would have to wonder what miracles you could perform if you were to create them in actual clay."

He turned the tiny square around in his fingers. "It's almost a shame to eat it." But then he popped it in his mouth. "But it's too delicious not to."

Andrew picked up another one of the petit fours. "I recognize these dogs. They're all from Applebottom," he said. "I'm sure their owners would kill to have these."

"They're portraits?" River practically squealed.

They were sure fussing over a few dog heads. "I do a set every few days," Sandy said. "When I don't have a big cake to decorate. It fills the hours."

"So that is the secret," River said. "Oodles of time. But so rare. I have to fight for my hours for art."

"Because of your classes?" Sandy asked.

"Because of the pressures of being River Montgomery," River said. "Oh, to be obscure again. To create incredibly detailed busts of doggies on cake." He picked up another one, this one with the largest dog in town, Roscoe, a Great Dane. He popped it in his mouth.

"Do the townspeople know you're creating their dogs on cakes?" Andrew asked.

"I don't know," Sandy said. "I'm not sure anybody's really noticed."

River smacked the table with both hands. "Please tell me you're taking photographs at least."

"I haven't felt the need to. I do them all the time." These little dog heads were not even close to her best work.

River scooted away from the table. "Grab your tea. We're going upstairs."

Andrew and Sandy did as instructed, picking up their cups and following River through the atrium. They went up a back set of stairs, these going straight to a landing on the second floor.

Here they walked along the carpeted hall, floor to ceiling with more art. These were mostly portraits, and Sandy could see that the styles were all over the place. More purchases by River.

They passed the opening that led to the curving stairs and down to the foyer. Sandy took a moment to peer over the railing at all the art downstairs. Amazing. She could have spent hours just walking through that foyer again and again.

She hurried to catch up with River and Andrew. River had opened another door just past the landing.

Another set of stairs, narrow and steep, led them to a most astonishing room.

The ceiling was a glass dome, and sunlight flooded

every inch of the space. It was the size of a typical class-room, scattered with tables and stools and easels. Shelves along one wall were filled with every manner of artistic tool. Paintbrushes. Canvases. Palettes. Stacks of textured paper. Collections of charcoal and pens and colored pencils and ink.

An entire section was devoted to various textiles, including broken pottery, glass beads, shells, and mosaic tiles.

"Is this where you work?" Sandy asked.

"It is my sanctuary," River said.

Sandy approached one of the tables, littered with brightly colored bits of glass. On one end, a small tub held a pretty rose-colored vase and a small metal hammer. This must be where he broke apart objects.

Seeing his work in progress flooded Sandy with a mixture of gratitude and disbelief. To meet an artist of River's caliber was one thing. But here she was getting to see where he worked. How he was inspired. It was almost too much.

"Come here, my girl," River said. He gestured her toward a long table to one side. It held every manner of sculpting material. Polymer. Air dry clay. Plaster gauze. Resins. Wire forms and rollers and carving toolsets.

"What sort of clay are you most comfortable with?" he asked.

"I've only ever used paper clay," Sandy said. She stopped herself from adding that resin was too expen-sive and dried too quickly.

"Fair enough." He reached beneath the table and brought out a box filled with every possible brand and color of paper clay. "I'll get you some water so that you can soften it. And some paints for coloring the clay."

Were they going to do something right then?

Sandy glanced at Andrew. "Do we have time for this?" They still had a four-hour drive back home.

"This is your day," Andrew said. "If we don't get back until midnight, well, we're adults."

Sandy opened a package of plain white mermaid clay. "You should do some, too." She handed him a blob of clay and showed him how to work it with his fingers to soften it. When River arrived with small bowls of water to help smooth the clay, she almost hummed contentedly as they all set to work.

"I assume you want me to do your puppy dogs," she said, glancing down at the little pack that had followed them throughout the house.

River sighed happily. "I was hoping you would offer."

And so they sculpted, the dogs for Sandy, with River working on some abstract object that looked a bit like a sea monster. And Andrew, well, she wasn't sure exactly what Andrew was trying to do. Possibly the world's ugliest worm.

It was pretty much the best day ever.

# CHAPTER 13

*A*ndrew rolled the car up to Sandy's house well past midnight

Sandy had chattered almost the entire drive home about River and his house and all the art there. She'd made miniature sculptures of all six of his dogs, and River had promised to keep them in a prominent location forever and ever.

Andrew couldn't stop smiling. Sandy seemed so happy, so aglow. As he killed the engine in front of her gravel driveway, she announced, "I don't feel the least bit sleepy!"

"That's good, since I'm sure Betty expects you to be at work on time."

Sandy clapped her hand over her mouth. "Oh, my gosh! You have to teach tomorrow! I kept you out way too late!"

"Correction, I believe River Montgomery kept us

late in the city four hours from home. But it's fine. I'll be fine."

"Are you sure? I feel like I should bring you extra strong coffee in the morning to make sure you can get through the day."

Andrew would have loved that, actually, but of course their relationship was nowhere near the point of having the intimacy of her bringing him coffee to work.

"I promise that I'll be fine. I can handle a single night being up late."

They sat in the car a minute more, just staring at each other in the moonlight, when Sandy jumped in her seat. "Oh! It's so late, and here I am keeping you longer. Thank you so much for today. What an amazing day. The best day. The best day ever."

Her absolute exuberance made him smile even bigger. "Me, too."

"Are you sure? I was so worried because we sat there for hours and hours talking about nothing but art styles and the best way to make a dog nose and how long before air dry clay would get too difficult to work with."

"It was perfect," he assured her.

Sandy reached for her door, and he jumped out to run around and open it for her. She gathered her sunglasses and her scarf in her bag, plus an entire box of extra clay that River had given her, promising that it would just go bad if he kept it.

"Let me help you with that," he said.

"No, I've got it," she insisted. In fact, she seemed a

little frazzled as she hurried toward her front door, almost as if she was trying to escape him.

"Is everything okay?"

He didn't follow her up the path. Something told him that perhaps she was concerned that he would try to force his way in or something.

She dumped everything at her doorstep and rushed back to him. "No! Not at all! I just. I…"

Whatever it was, he didn't want to make the end of this evening hard for her in any way. "I guess I'll see you at our next centennial meeting," he said. "Unless you wanted to do something before. Maybe dinner in Branson?"

"That would be lovely," she said. "This weekend?"

His chest relaxed. So whatever was going on a minute ago, it didn't have to do with him. At least not directly. "Should I pick you up around six on Saturday? That would give us time to get there."

"Yes. Sounds perfect."

His heart sped up. There was only maybe two feet between them, but he faltered in bridging the gap to kiss her good night. He wasn't sure why. He wanted to do it. She seemed receptive, smiling up at him in the moonlight.

But he didn't want to rush things. This had to be new to her. He'd seen no evidence that she had dated anyone in the timeframe since she left high school. Better to take things easy than to mess it up. He'd already closed the deal on a second date. He would quit while he was ahead.

As a compromise, he lifted her fingers to his lips for a gentle kiss. "I look forward to it, Sandy."

He held onto her hand for a few long beats, then released her.

As he pulled away from her house, she waited on the porch, watching him drive away. It had been a long day, but an amazing one.

Everything about Sandy Miller felt like coming home.

In the end, Andrew discovered he couldn't wait all the way until Saturday to see Sandy again. He drove down to Town Square after school on Thursday, stopping at Applebottom Blossoms to pick up a small bouquet of flowers before heading down to Tea for Two.

When he walked into the tea shop, however, his heart sank to see Sandy's cake decorating table cleared and empty.

Betty sat on her stool behind the counter. "I'm guessing those lovely flowers are not for me."

"Sandy not working today?"

"I would leave Sandy to tell it, but it's already all over town," Betty said. "I'm surprised Sadie didn't march down to your room to tell you what happened."

Every muscle in Andrew's body tensed. This sounded bad. "Is she okay?"

"That depends on what you call okay," Betty said. "That baby daddy decided to step out from that rock he's been hiding under and exert some paternal influence over the boy."

"Jerry Lavinski?"

Betty shifted uncomfortably on her stool. "It would appear so," she said with a frown. "Funny that when he was asked to take responsibility for what he did eighteen years ago, he insisted he had nothing to do with child. But now that the boy's showing promise in college football, he wants to be involved."

"Caden is an adult. What can his father do?"

"That I don't know. But it must be something. Sandy ran out of here like her skirt was on fire."

"Thank you, Betty." Andrew turned to leave the tea shop. "Did she say when she'd be back?"

"Not a word."

As Andrew walked back to his car, the flowers still in his hand, he wondered if he should call Sandy. Or text her. They'd exchanged numbers after the first centennial meeting. But until now, they had always met face-to-face to make decisions. It seemed presumptuous of him to write her about this. But at the same time, he wanted to help her if she needed it.

He sat in his car a good ten minutes, phone in hand, trying to decide what to do. It was high school all over again. Only now, the stakes were higher. Sandy had a son. And apparently the boy's father was still around. No one had known that. Sandy hadn't mentioned it.

Now that he thought of it, how had Sandy supported herself all these years, living out of town with no job and the sick mother who had eventually passed away?

Even if the mother had provided some sort of income, it ended years ago. Sandy had skirted the issue when River brought it up. This whole situation made one thing clear to Andrew. As much as he liked her, he didn't really know her at all.

In the end, he set his phone down, instead scrawling a simple note on a piece of paper. He left the note and the flowers on Sandy's door.

If she wanted to let him in on her secrets, he would be waiting.

# CHAPTER 14

Sandy tried her hardest to coax her mother's ancient Ford Focus to climb over sixty miles an hour as she buzzed down the highway between Applebottom and the community college where her son played football.

She couldn't believe that jerk Jerry Lavinksi had reentered Caden's life at this point.

But she should have known.

Caden was exactly the sort of son that made fathers proud. Charming, good-looking, athletic.

Maybe it was petty, but Sandy didn't want Jerry to have a piece of her son. He hadn't been there for the nights of no sleep, the diaper changes, the banged-up knees, the broken arm in fourth grade, or his failing to pass algebra, requiring summer school. All the heartaches, large and small, and especially those moments where a father would have given him a guiding hand, had been hers to bear.

She had done it all, even while living in near poverty and under the thumb of a mean-spirited mother. She kept going even when her mother died, and Sandy had to go it completely alone, isolated from everyone to keep the secret that Jerry was now telling the world.

If only she hadn't taken the hush money, eighteen years worth of quarterly payments to raise the kid and say nothing.

But who was she kidding? Her own father had left them. Her mother had worked cleaning houses until she was too sick to do it anymore. There was no way she could have raised Caden without Jerry's family's money.

And she'd done right by him. He was in college! Neither Sandy nor either of her parents had managed to finish high school. Maybe it wasn't any big fancy school, but with Jerry's money cut off right as he graduated, they didn't have a ton of options. The full scholarship to play football on this little team had been a Godsend. Academics weren't Caden's strong suit, and this junior college would enable him to learn a trade with football paying the way.

Surely Jerry didn't think Caden had a future in pro ball. Caden was talented, but his experience was very limited, coming from a tiny school like Applebottom.

She knew exactly what had prompted Jerry to call, though. He'd seen that fumble and video of Caden from the first game. It was the sort of clip that got passed around and Caden's full name had been on it, as well as the school where he played.

So Jerry had come. He wanted a little bit of his shunned child's fame.

Oh, that made her so angry.

Surely by now he had his own family, a wife, and other children that he wasn't shocked or embarrassed by.

But Jerry was no doubt the same snake-charming liar that he had been as a teenager. No doubt Caden would be starstruck. Jerry was his father, after all.

Sandy didn't know what to do. Caden deserved to know his father, good, bad or ugly. The whole thing just filled her with fear. And if she admitted it in her heart of hearts, the big worry was that she would lose him, that Jerry would convince him to move so far away, that Sandy couldn't jump in the car and see her son. Jerry had family with money and connections that could turn a young man's head. And all the years that Sandy had spent would be erased.

The college was only a half hour east of Branson, and she felt as though she had barely collected her thoughts when she arrived at the tiny campus.

It was nothing like the University of Missouri, but it did have a collection of sturdy buildings, a student center, and a dormitory where Caden lived.

She pulled into a visitor spot and hurried toward the dorm, texting Caden that she was there.

He wrote back to say that he was downstairs in the

lounge, and to brace herself, because Jerry was still there.

For the first time since she realized Jerry had found their son, Sandy stopped to consider her appearance. She didn't want to walk in looking like a harried spinster who had failed at life.

Thankfully, because of Andrew's regular visits in the shop, lately she always cleaned up a little, putting on lip gloss and making sure her outfits were pressed and looked the best they could. Her brown skirt was simple, and the white sweater a little thin, but she was respectable.

She smoothed her hair and hurried up the walkway to the dorm. Facing Jerry after eighteen years was not something she had ever expected she would have to do.

Time to confront her past.

Jerry and Caden sat together on the sofa in the lobby of Caden's dorm.

The eighteen years had changed Jerry, but she would've known him anywhere. His sandy brown hair was still the same color as his son's. While Caden was growing up, Sandy hadn't thought that he looked like his father. But seeing them side-by-side, she had to admit the resemblance was quite striking. They had the same angular nose and square jaw. When they both looked up, Sandy's breath caught at the similarity in their somewhat grim expressions.

Of course, with the time that had passed, Jerry was clearly no longer an athlete. His Georgia Tech sweatshirt stretched over a belly paunch. He sat leaning forward with his elbows on his knees, hands clasped together.

"Hey, Mom," Caden said, his head hanging low, and instantly Sandy's maternal senses went on alert.

Jerry's eyes narrowed, as if he were prepping for a battle.

"Hello, Caden," she said to her son, then shifted to his father. "Jerry."

In the moments while he stared at her, unspeaking, Sandy sorted through every conversation she'd had with Caden about his father, assuming they'd all been discussed while the two of them waited for her.

Naturally, Caden had asked who his father was and where he might be. Sandy kept her answers simple. He was someone she had only known for a little while, and he had moved away. It hadn't made sense to explain the hush money, the payments, her inability to name the father or counteract the lies spread by him. That was too much for a child.

If Caden had heard other things in his years in Applebottom, he had not shared them with her.

But even now, sitting beside his flesh-and-blood father, she did not sense that Caden was angry with her for failing to disclose this information. Now that she had arrived, his face had relaxed, his hands loosely clasped, a position that mirrored his father.

Sandy sat down on a chair adjacent to the sofa, trying to stuff down the feeling that she might throw up. When Jerry still didn't say anything, as if all his words were huge secrets not to be trusted to her, she decided to just keep going. "So Caden, how are your classes going?"

"Fine," he said. "I'm doing all right."

"Practices going well?"

"Yeah. Coach says I'll probably play more this weekend."

Now Jerry sprang to life. "Exactly! The boy is bigger than this pathetic school. I've already called the coaches at three of the schools I attended," he said. "He's a legacy. He ought to be playing with the big dogs."

Sandy stuffed down her first reaction, which was to throttle him, and coolly asked, "You attended three schools? Did they kick you out of the first two?"

She had struck home. Jerry's face colored purple. "You've holed this boy up in smallville. He was destined to be great. He's my son, after all."

Caden's eyes shifted to the floor. He surely didn't know what to make of this man who had come out of nowhere with his blustery proclamations.

"These are Caden's decisions to make," Sandy said carefully. But she did not take the edge out of her voice. She wanted Jerry to know that she was not the shy, fumbling girl she had been at fifteen.

Or even a couple months ago. Decorating in Betty's shop, seeing her work in a newspaper, and now, after a glimpse of what normal dating life with a nice man looked like, she felt strong. Jerry could do nothing to her. Not anymore.

"The boy's still wet behind the ears, and he's obviously been coddled by his mother," Jerry spit out.

"Caden is a smart, capable young man," Sandy countered. "You don't get to waltz in here after eighteen years and derail all the progress we've made over his life. You didn't earn that."

"But I paid for it," he said. "You got money for this boy. It's about time I got to see a return on my investment."

Sandy shot up from her chair. "He's your son, not a piece of real estate. And I find it very interesting you are willing to claim him now that he's a football player."

"Mom!" Caden said. "Enough!" He turned to Jerry. "I appreciate you coming down here to meet me. I've always wondered who you were. But you don't get to tell me what to do. And I'm an adult now. Legally, you have no say in my future."

Sandy's heart swelled with pride. Caden was strong. He had found his way. She had done right by her son.

The color in Jerry's face moved all the way into the roots of his thinning hair. "As your parent, I can go to the Dean of the School and unenroll you."

Sandy took a step closer to Jerry. "Actually, the terms of the contract were that I could not list you on the birth certificate. So until you get a lawyer and have it legally changed, you are no one to me, to Caden, and certainly not to the officials at this school."

Jerry's mouth opened, then closed. "I'm his father. You and I both know it."

"You certainly didn't think so at the time. You said maybe it was the whole basketball team."

Caden's faced colored pink. "Mom…"

"That's what he told everyone." She would not let Jerry upset the well-thought-out plan she and Caden had put together.

Jerry's eyes narrowed. "I'll take the contract to them. It'll show that I'm the father."

"Go right ahead," Sandy said, her voice low. "But you only get to see him if he wants that. And if he doesn't, I'll be glad to help him get a restraining order taken out on you."

Jerry stood up. "You wouldn't dare."

Sandy took one step back and gestured to the visitor's desk, where a wide-eyed woman sat with her hand on the phone.

"Literally one wave from me, and she calls the police, I'm pretty sure once they hear the situation, they're not going to be on your side."

Jerry stalked toward the door. When he had made it about halfway across the room, he turned back to them. "This isn't over. That is my son, and I am going to guide him to be the person I think he should be. And that's not some half-baked second stringer on a pointless junior college football team. I have every intention of showing up at the next football game with a recruiter and new options for *my son*."

Sandy wasn't going to let him take off with the last word. "Maybe if you had been around, he could've gone to one of the schools that kicked *you* out. But at this point, Caden gets to decide how much involvement you have in his life. He'll call you. Don't call him."

When Jerry had safely exited the door, Sandy turned to her son. "You okay? I had no idea he would do that. None. I haven't heard from him one time since his family forced me to leave Applebottom."

"He made you leave?"

"Yes." Sandy sank back into her chair. She waved at the woman by the telephone to show they were all right.

It was time to come clean with her son.

"Your father didn't want anything to do with me once I got pregnant. He told everyone in Applebottom that the baby wasn't his. One day, his father—your grandfather—came to our house with a lawyer. His family does have a fair amount of money. They offered to pay me to raise you, if I would never tell anyone, even you, the identity of your father."

Caden's gaze had dropped to the floor again. This was a lot to take in. "And you agreed to that?"

"I didn't know what else to do. I was fifteen years old. We were poor. Nonna worked as a housecleaner. We barely got by. His money enabled me to raise you without having to get a job. And when Nonna got sick and couldn't work, it literally saved us."

"I hope you don't think I should be grateful to them," Caden said.

"I don't. It was a dastardly thing to do, to refuse to claim you, and then to say such terrible things about me. But it's in the past now. I'm back in town, and I work in the square. The town has let bygones be bygones. So have I. So can you."

"He can't really tell the Dean to take me out, can he?"

"I don't think so," Sandy said. "He has no proof he's your father, and even if he did, I'm not certain he could do anything with you being over eighteen. But to make sure, I will go there myself to let them know that there's a bit of a situation."

Caden set up, tugging at the bottom of his T-shirt. He looked young and vulnerable, despite being the size of a full-grown man. Sandy's eyes pricked with tears as she looked at him, all the hurt that he had to carry.

"At least now you know that he's out there," she said. "If at some point you feel like you've outgrown this small college, or if some bigger college does come knocking, he's certainly a resource. Just know exactly how much you can trust him. And always question what his motivations might be for helping you."

Caden rubbed his hand across his head. It was late afternoon, but he seemed tired.

"Early morning practice?" Sandy asked.

"Every day."

"When's your next class?"

"Twenty minutes," Caden said.

"You should go grab your things then," she said. "I'll stop by the Dean's office. Don't worry."

She stood up. Caden embraced her in a long hug.

"Thank you for coming, Mom," he said. "I'm sorry I dragged you all the way over here."

"No, you did the right thing. It's just an hour drive. I can leave the tea shop. Betty is perfectly capable of watching over it herself."

"As she's done for a hundred years," Caden said.

Sandy smiled. "Exactly."

She sent him back upstairs and headed over to the woman at the desk to assure her that things were fine and ask directions to the Dean's office.

Jerry Lavinski. She never thought she would see him again. But he was back.

# CHAPTER 15

On the drive back to Applebottom, Sandy's shock wore off and a slow burn of anger began to build. She repeatedly smacked the steering wheel and railed at Jerry Lavinski. How dare he show up in their lives right now? How dare he threaten Caden's future? How dare he try to force his involvement in Caden's life at this late date?

And of course, now there was the subject of Saturday. Caden had an away game she'd planned to skip in favor of the first one at the home field. But Jerry's threat to show up and disrupt Caden's place on the team meant Sandy really needed to go and intervene.

She would have to cancel her date with Andrew.

What was she doing dating Andrew anyway? She couldn't even confess about what had actually happened eighteen years ago. Hush money and contracts and how she'd basically sold her silence. She was keeping this huge secret from him, from the entire town.

What she really needed to do was make an entirely fresh start. Wasn't that what Andrew had told her? Dream big. Maybe that was exactly what needed to happen. Get out of this town. Get away from the old ghosts.

If she put her mind to it, she could take the little extra money she had right now and invest it into her sad little house. She'd use her artistic skill to make it something cute and interesting. Or trendy. Or something. If she got enough money out of it, she could move to St. Louis, or, gosh, California. Or, New York. Why not? Somewhere completely different.

No, she couldn't go that far from Caden. But she could definitely go other directions. There was Fayetteville. Springfield. Columbia.

Thinking of the city where Andrew had taken her made her stomach drop. She needed to nip this right now. She had to give up on what they'd started.

She'd turned away from Andrew when she was fifteen years old. She could do it again.

Andrew sat in his car a while, looking at the text from Sandy one more time in the vain hope that he'd somehow read it wrong the first time.

*Andrew – must cancel dinner on Saturday. Must cancel*

*everything. Life got complicated. Sorry. I will still make the cake for the centennial.*

He'd driven across town the moment school let out to talk to her about it. But then he'd only gotten as far as the parking lot on Town Square. He wasn't sure he had the nerve to walk into Tea for Two.

And he didn't know if he *should* anyway.

Something had gone on between Sandy and Jerry, something that made Sandy rush to Caden's junior college. But the cryptic note didn't explain why she was pulling away from him.

The message was so simple, he couldn't figure out any context from it. Did this mean Jerry had changed her heart? Were they going to see each other now? Raise Caden together? Celebrate his football career?

Or was she in some sort of trouble again? Had Jerry Lavinski derailed her life again, eighteen years later?

Andrew had let her go before and regretted it. There was no way he was going to do it again, not with this second chance they'd been given.

He would fight for her.

With this new surge of certainty, Andrew got out of his car and walked swiftly down the street to Betty's tea shop.

The bell jingled as he entered. There were no customers in the shop, and Sandy's table was empty. In fact, it was shoved in the corner, and the padded chair she had been using was no longer in the main room at all. It looked as though Betty no longer intended to have Sandy decorate out there.

What did that mean? Did Sandy quit her job? Was she moving somewhere?

His heart thudded. Had Jerry stolen her away from him again?

"I figured you'd be darkening my door," Betty said from her stool behind the counter. "Can I get you some Applebottom tea?"

Andrew nodded as he headed toward the counter.

Betty slid off the seat and moved to the hot water spigot with pained slowness. Clementine was with her today, curled up on a little miniature throne beneath the sink.

"Is everything okay?" Andrew asked. He really wanted to ask about Sandy, but propriety forced him to give it a minute.

"Depends on what you call okay." She filled a cup with hot water and opened the canister marked with her special tea blend.

Andrew glanced at the door to the back. He strained his ears, but he heard nothing.

"She's here, if that's what you're worried about," Betty said. "But I can't let you back there. She's asked to be left to her work."

"Am I allowed to even know what happened?"

Betty passed him the steaming mug. "I reckon if she wants to talk about it, she'll do it herself."

"But she still works here? She's not moving away?"

"She still works here, son," Betty said, her expression softening. "You bide your time. Sometimes life has its complications, but they have their way of working themselves out."

He couldn't help but ask. "Does she seem okay, though?"

"She's fine. We'll take good care of her."

Andrew looked down at the insulated to-go cup she had passed him. Normally he got a ceramic mug that meant *sit and talk a while*. Clearly, this one meant he needed to leave.

He pulled his wallet out to pay for the tea, but Betty waved him away. "On the house, of course."

"Thank you." He turned for the door. "Will you tell her I came to see her?"

"I'm sure she knows," Betty said. "The shop isn't that big."

Andrew headed out onto the sidewalk. A gust of wind sent leaves skittering across the sidewalk and brought on a sudden chill.

He kept his head down. How quickly optimism could be chased away, just like the warm sunny days of summer giving way to fall.

He would do what Betty suggested. Ride it out. Give her a little space.

Applebottom was a small town. If anything happened that meant Sandy was lost to him forever, he would know it soon enough.

❧

When Andrew was gone, Sandy leaned against the doorframe between the back room and the tea shop. Betty had settled back on her stool.

"How was he?" Sandy asked.

"He looked a little dejected, as you might expect."

Betty adjusted herself on her seat. Clementine lifted her head from her little bed and cast a bleary glance at the two of them, and set it down again.

"For the record, I think you're making a mistake," Betty said. "I don't know what happened between you and that character who caused you so much grief. But Andrew is a good man, so make sure you treat him that way."

A lump formed in Sandy's throat. "Things are just too complicated right now to date somebody. I have to think of Caden."

"Caden is a young adult now," Betty said. "It's high time that you started thinking about your life. What *you* want."

Sandy turned back to Fierce's sweet sixteen cake, which was slowly coming together. She'd spaced out the hard frosting pieces and practiced attaching them to a sample cake. She would be delivering this one on Friday. She sort of looked forward to that. Black decorations, doom, gloom. It sounded like the perfect backdrop to her life as she was living it right now.

*A*ndrew sat in the conference room at the high school as nervous as he'd ever been. The centennial celebration committee would be meeting, and he wasn't sure if Sandy would show or not.

This time, it would not just be the two of them. The school secretary had taken his notes on the history of Applebottom and run with them, recruiting several people from town to host various booths that would be set up in the school cafeteria. The citizens of Applebottom would get a sample of all the things that had made their town unique as it celebrated the school's one hundredth anniversary.

Clearly, he was just a figurehead, and the meetings had been to put him with Sandy. The real work of the centennial was being done by Sadie.

Fine by him.

Within minutes of his arrival, Gertrude and Maude showed up with samples of the pie they were going to provide at their booth.

They were quickly followed by Janine, who owned the town's nail salon and spa. She had put together little packets of her signature Applebottom hand cream to give out at the celebration.

Topher and Danny arrived next with the drawings of the bouquets and a large topiary arch they would be constructing around the entrance, using plants and cuttings from the native trees in the area.

Even the town mayor, T-bone, had showed up in his usual black leather motorcycle vest complete with patches, a long grizzly beard, and heavy boots. He would be giving a speech.

They were all happily munching on miniature pies when the band director rushed in, plucking at his navy blazer and apologizing for being late.

"I have the marching band practicing a couple extra songs from the era," he said. "Is the plan for us to march in during the middle of the festivities? Or do you want us to lead everyone in at the start?"

Gertrude brushed her hands free of crumbs and said, "I think it will be fine for them to come in partway through. It would be a grand entrance and get everyone's attention just in time for T-bone to speak."

Andrew nodded. They were pretty much running the meeting without him. It was just as well, since his mind couldn't focus on anything but Sandy. They were twenty minutes in, and their cake decorator had not shown up.

Maude passed a tray of pies down to the band director. "It's my understanding that someone will be rolling out the cake," she said. "And that it needs an explanation because it is so elaborate."

The committee turned to him. "Right," he said. "Sandy really wasn't up for getting up to talk about the cake, but I was going to explain it from the historical standpoint."

"Very good," Maude said. "So it sounds like we'll open the door to vendors around six, and then maybe around six forty-five the band will come in. At 7 o'clock, the mayor will speak. Then roll out the cake. You will talk a little bit about the significance. Then everyone will eat cake and it's over."

"Sounds good to me," Andrew said.

"Has anyone seen this cake of hers?" Gertrude asked with a bite in her voice. "I still think a pie is more important than a cake for a town named after a pie."

"Hush," Maude said. "Nobody cares. You can't put the history of the town on a pie."

Andrew shifted in his chair. "I've seen the sketches," he said. "It will be amazing."

"Good enough," Maude said, shushing Gertrude.

After that, the meeting devolved into chatter. Andrew sat at the head of the table, feeling removed from it all.

Eventually, a voice cut through the noise to capture his attention. "Where is Sandy, anyway?" Danny asked.

"I'm not sure that girl is as devoted to Applebottom as she ought to be," Janine said.

Andrew tried not to bristle at the accusation. He wanted to say, *And why should she be, after the way all of you treated her years ago?* But he didn't.

Janine still wore her pink smock from her work at the spa. Seeing a smear of cooled wax marring her sleeve gave him a small sense of justice as she and Gertrude nodded knowingly.

Maude pushed the tray of pies at Janine. "Might be best if you filled that mouth with something sweet."

Andrew coughed over his laugh. These people definitely had their quirks. If he had to pick, though, Maude would be his favorite. She'd saved Applebottom Pie Shoppe from closing by buying out half, and kept the curmudgeonly Gertrude in line. The two of them could not have been any more devoted to Applebottom, even if they were as different as peas and turnips—a favorite expression of Maude's.

He sat back in his chair. No sense drawing this meeting out until it became pure gossip. "Sounds like it's all under control. I'll make sure the cafeteria is unlocked so everyone can set up. Meeting adjourned."

Everyone took one last pie from Maude's tray and filed out. Andrew waited for all of them to leave before picking up his folder and shouldering his bag. The room was quiet, the halls going still again.

He glanced at the chair where Sandy had sat the first time and wondered how he could get them back to where they had been.

Maybe it wasn't possible.

# CHAPTER 17

*A*s Sandy chugged along the highway to the obscure little football stadium where Caden would be playing his second college football game, she practiced all the things she might say to Jerry Lavinski when she saw him again.

He wouldn't be taking her by surprise this time. She would say all the things that she wished she'd said in the eighteen years she'd raised their son alone.

As the miles passed by, Sandy wished she had Andrew with her. Even though this drive was only two hours compared to the four she spent with him going to Columbia, it seemed to pass much more slowly.

She'd botched that, she knew. But while this problem raged with Jerry, she couldn't subject a new relationship to it. Besides, she was just as aware as everyone else about what it looked like, to once again ditch Andrew for something Jerry had done. Why did her history have to keep repeating itself?

After what felt like three days, she pulled up to the football stadium. She was ridiculously early, because she wanted to take no chance that Jerry might show up and try to bully his way into the field house before the game.

She wished she had followed him outside a few days ago to see what sort of car he drove. No doubt it would be fancy. His family came from a long line of car dealers. Maybe that was why they were so good at convincing people to do things they shouldn't. They treated every part of their lives like a sale that needed to be closed.

Only fifty or so cars sat in the lot at this point. The team itself had arrived on buses. The idea that Caden still occasionally rode a little yellow school bus made her smile. Poor college. They didn't even have enough money to upgrade the transportation for the team.

But they were doing the important part — covering her son's tuition.

She took a few minutes to wander the parking lot, looking at each vehicle. She seemed to remember from back in the day that Jerry's family always had decals announcing their dealership on their cars. They missed no opportunity to advertise. A quick walk in the crisp, cool air assured her that unless something had changed, Jerry's car was not there yet.

Good. He couldn't do anything unexpected without her being there to mitigate his actions.

Another bus arrived, this one holding the cheerleaders. Then the band. The early spectators started to arrive, and the ticket booth window opened. Sandy kept her eye on the field house as she paid her admission and entered the stadium. It seemed unlikely any coach would let a random father, much less a father unwanted by a player, to infiltrate the pregame meeting while they were suiting up.

She settled on a low bench on the visitors' side, almost completely alone, as workers organized the sideline equipment.

The weather was beautiful for football. Cool but not cold. The late afternoon sun warmed Sandy's face. From beneath the stands, popcorn began popping, and the smell made her stomach grumble. Since the team had not even taken the field for warm-up yet, she hurried down to the concession stand and bought some hot chocolate and popcorn. When she returned, a few other fans were sprinkled throughout the seats, waiting for the players to emerge.

A friendly couple maybe ten years older than her walked across the stands, holding hands. Once again, Sandy regretted not having Andrew with her. He would've been totally happy to show up and see the football game rather than have dinner in Branson. He just wanted to do something with her.

She really had messed up. But what could she have done differently? For all she knew, Jerry and his entire family were about to show up and make a big spectacle in the stands. No, this was something she had to do alone. She needed to see the whole problem through, and then maybe she could rethink her plan. Maybe she didn't have to leave Applebottom.

The home side had considerably more spectators arrive early, and they all stood to cheer as their team ran out on the field for the warm up.

The couple she'd spotted clapped politely for the opposing team. Sandy tried to set aside her anxiety about Jerry and enjoy the moment.

Sitting low in the stands was new. For Caden's four years in football, she had climbed to the top corners, keeping to herself. But here, no one around her knew her history. They wouldn't look down on her or whisper about how she'd gotten pregnant as a sophomore in high school.

She sat up a little straighter. She didn't need to leave Applebottom to start over. Her fresh start was right here. With her son.

Caden's team ran onto the field, and Sandy jumped to her feet with an exuberance she'd never felt brave enough to show in her hometown.

She shouted. She clapped. She might have screamed a little. A handful of students from the college rushed into the stands, all decked in Fisher Junior College green and gold. They sat near her, adding to the noise. Sandy wanted to laugh out loud. This was *fun*.

The tiny band clunked up the metal steps to fill in the space to her right. The cheerleaders ran out onto the track in front of the stands. Sandy felt exuberant. She could almost have been one of the students. She unbuttoned her coat to show off the T-shirt Caden had given her.

As the team began their stretches and the general furor died down, the older couple scooted closer to her. "You look like a football mom," the woman said. She extended a hand. "I'm Shannon. This is Bill. Our son Tanner plays for Fisher. Does yours?"

Sandy actually felt her eyes prick with pride as she said, "Yes. My son is Caden Miller. He's just a freshman."

Bill leaned forward, adjusting the brim of his green and gold ball cap. "He's the fella that had that viral video from the last game, isn't he?"

Sandy nodded. "He called me about it that night. Pretty crazy recovery."

"I'll say," Shannon said. "I think he's going to advance pretty fast. If Fisher isn't careful, some four-year college will snatch him up."

"You think so?" Sandy hadn't considered that Jerry could be right. Maybe Caden was better than she realized.

"It happens all the time," Shannon said. "Tanner says half the team is trying to make big plays to get noticed."

"I was just pleased that he got his tuition paid," Sandy said.

"It's definitely a perk," Shannon said. "These boys

always want to go pro. But that's like lightning in a bottle."

The band struck up a number, playing so loud that it made conversation impossible. Contentment washed over Sandy as she watched Caden zigzag with sprints across the field. He'd found a place where he belonged. Where he had potential. And where he could be seen. If more came of it, that was great. If not, he would still get the degree, and a head start on his future.

This was all she could really ask for in life. To have a child and watch him succeed.

Although, a little tickle in her belly said that there was more. There was family. There was connection.

And, possibly, there could be love.

She ate popcorn and chatted with Bill and Shannon between band numbers, until the players left the field again in preparation for kickoff.

Sandy watched warily for Jerry and possibly his entourage, but so far, nothing. She had no idea where he lived now. Had he taken a flight to see Caden earlier this week?

As the pregame events began with announcements and drill teams and people hocking programs, Sandy began to relax. Maybe they had been idle threats. And maybe, just maybe, he'd been surprised by how strong she was, and got scared off.

The stands filled up, and the teams came back out to the announcer's enthusiastic introductions and the coin toss.

A whistle signaled kickoff, and Sandy spotted Caden on the sideline, hopping up and down and cheering on his team. He was a good sport. He didn't have to be the star. But she noticed that teammates and sideline crew kept coming up to talk to him. Like in Applebottom, he was popular and friendly. He would do well.

As the clock kept ticking, Sandy got more and more into the game. As the Fisher Dragons pulled ahead, she and Shannon frequently turned to hug each other. This was what parenting was all about. Shared experiences with other families. Finding your tribe.

As the game continued with no sign of Jerry, Sandy felt transformed. She would go to *all* the games. Who cared if they were home or away. None of them were more than three or four hours to drive. This was her new passion. She no longer had to feel afraid. She would meet the other parents. She would become involved in something. And opportunities would certainly come along as she increased her willingness to put herself out there and connect to others.

Shannon squeezed her arm. "They're putting Caden in!"

Sandy scanned the field. Sure enough, Caden was trotting out to the twenty-yard line, where the team had just signaled fair catch after a punt.

Tanner high-fived Caden as they set up for their first play.

Shannon elbowed Sandy. "Looks like our boys get along."

A warm rush of emotion coursed through Sandy yet again. She felt so filled to the brim with happiness that she wasn't sure her body could contain it. She'd felt close to this at Caden's graduation, and then again when he got word of the scholarship to Fisher.

But this wasn't just about him. It was her, too. She was here, among people with common interests. Coming so soon after her amazing weekend with Andrew and River, Sandy wondered if she had even lived before this day. The air was sweeter, colors brighter. She'd just been in such a hole for so long.

The play began, and Caden made a clean snap to Tanner. Tanner fell back, looking as though he would throw a long pass, then secretly handed off to one of the receivers. The fake worked, and the Dragons gained twelve yards and another first down.

Sandy and their entire side of the stadium jumped to their feet. As the drive resulted in a touchdown, solidifying Fisher's lead, Sandy started yelling herself hoarse. There was nothing like this feeling, nothing.

As the clock wound down, and Caden was able to stay in for the rest of the game, Sandy felt exultant. Jerry hadn't showed. Yet another threat that amounted to nothing. If only Sandy had known eighteen years ago how little follow-through he had. She could have lived her life, finished high school, done so much more. But she had been living in fear.

No more.

As the band played the school song, and the team

linked arms and the cheerleaders sang, Sandy knew that she had overreacted to Jerry's arrival earlier that week. She didn't have to leave Applebottom to find her way or make a fresh start. She was already doing it.

Shannon grabbed her arm, and they hurried down to where the football players would file out to the field house. As they cheered their boys, Sandy knew what she had to do.

She had to make a cake. And maybe decorate it a little differently from what she had planned.

And probably she would have to talk in front of a lot of people.

People who had once judged her. Failed to help. Let her suffer.

But she wasn't doing this for herself.

It was for one other person.

One very special man.

She could do it.

The centennial celebration was going well.

Andrew stood against the wall, his arms crossed, feeling somewhat removed from the festivities. There was so much more going on than they had even discussed in the last meeting. Clearly some other group had actually been planning the thing. It didn't matter. The first meeting had done what it needed to do: forced him and Sandy together, if only for a little while.

Andrew had heard from the school secretary, who had talked to Delilah, who talked to Betty, that Sandy had canceled their dinner date to go to a football game and watch Caden. Jerry was nowhere in the picture.

That was a relief. Caden had gotten more play time this week than last. Andrew was happy for them. He really was.

He just didn't know where this left him. When they had been in Columbia, he felt for sure that Sandy wanted to keep seeing him. She'd even agreed to another date. But if she'd changed her mind now, he had no choice but to let her be.

All around him, booths bustled with visitors coming to sample the town's wares. Gertrude and Maude passed out miniature pies. Janine had her lotion samples. Danny and Topher were pinning tiny corsages on all of the women. They had really outdone themselves, doing this in addition to all the decorations.

Delilah had shown up with doggy treats for those who had pets. Not that the pets were in the cafeteria. Andrew suspected she had lobbied for that, but certainly made no headway.

Even grumpy old Arnold, the barber on Town Square, had showed up with a chair and clippers. He was wrangling any of the kids with unruly hair and trimming them up.

Andrew glanced at his watch. The marching band was due to enter any moment. Until then, a small quartet of old-timers was playing in the corner. One of the four was Alfred Felmont, the wealthiest man in Applebottom, rarely seen out and about. He played his violin with his eyes closed, joy relaxing his features. Andrew glanced over at the pie booth. Gertrude was well-known in town for harboring a multi-decade crush on the man. But today she was too busy with her pies to moon over him.

Unrequited affection. Andrew knew it well. For the first time, he felt a connection with Gertrude. She often came across as mean-spirited, even though she loved this town beyond reason. But he realized now that her curmudgeonly behavior sprang from harboring a bruised heart for too many years.

Perhaps what he had said to Sandy applied him, too. Maybe he should trust that the town would look after his mother. During that difficult time after his father died and his mother was so unwell, he was necessary. But now she was doing fine.

He looked over the crowd until he spotted her, sitting on a chair along the wall with several women from town. Each balanced a half-eaten plate of pie on their laps, and they laughed and cut up in a way that made him smile.

Maybe this school year would be his last. If he started putting in applications in January, he could see what was out there for the next school term. He might have to backtrack a bit, take some adjunct job. But it would be his old plan.

T-bone walked up, holding a plate with no fewer than three pies.

"How did you score three free samples?" Andrew said. "I got one early on, and they shooed me away when I tried to get another an hour later."

"It pays to be the mayor." T-bone shoved another bite of peach pie in his mouth, somehow miraculously avoiding all the wild, wiry bristles of his mustache and beard.

"It sure didn't pay to be the chair of the committee for this very event."

T-bone laughed. "If you're not one of them"—he gestured at the booths—"then you're just a figurehead."

"Mr. Mayor, are you saying that you're a figurehead?"

He shrugged and took another bite.

Andrew leaned in. "You may not know this, but those women are actually afraid of you."

T-bone stuck his plastic fork straight up in one of the uneaten pies and stroked his beard. "Yeah, I like it that way. Don't let anyone know that I might be a softy."

The room brightened as the broad side doors opened. A hush fell over the crowd. Just outside, the Applebottom High School marching band waited for their signal.

Andrew might be a figurehead, but he was still the person who had made the events move forward tonight.

He threaded his way through the crowd and climbed onto the stage to the microphone.

"Hello, everyone," he said. "Thank you for coming. I believe next up we have some traditional numbers performed by our own high school band!"

Someone did a count-off, and then the noise crashed through the room. Andrew flipped off the microphone and stepped back to watch. The festivities were at a peak. Most everyone in Applebottom was already here. After the band marched through and played, T-bone would speak. Then they would have the cake.

Wait. The cake.

Was it here? He hadn't seen it yet.

What if Sandy didn't come?

No, she'd said she would do the cake. She was the type of person who kept her word.

Of course, she could always send Betty.

He'd heard nothing about how the cake turned out. When Sandy had made the sketches, they'd agreed that some of their ideas might not fit exactly as they expected.

But if Sandy had made any adjustments, it had been without his input.

One of the high school students emerged from behind the curtain and whispered, "Mr. McAllister."

He stepped closer. "Everything okay?"

"Sandy said to tell you that the cake is here."

So she *was* here.

Andrew slid behind the curtain. Sandy directed several students to set boxes on the ground while she pushed a silver cart to center stage.

She wore a deep blue dress, spot on for Applebottom's school colors, and the scarf he had given her, tied smartly around her neck. His throat tightened at the sight of it. At least she was practical, continuing to wear the scarf even if it no longer held any sentimental value about him giving it to her.

Perhaps it never did.

She cut away the box on the cart, revealing the

bottom tier of the cake. Only when she turned to look for the next tier did she glance up and see him.

"It will only take me a moment to assemble the cake," she said.

No *hello*. No wavering of her expression. She was all business.

Andrew stood a little straighter. He'd match her for professionalism. "There's still plenty of time. The band will play four songs and then the mayor will speak."

She laughed and a bit of his resolved crumbled. He'd missed being near her.

"I hear our illustrious mayor is not big on words," she said. "I don't expect that part to last more than ninety seconds."

"Can I help you then?"

"All hands on deck!"

The first number ended and the crowd on the other side of the curtain clapped. As the next song began, she took a large box from a teen boy and passed it to Andrew. "Hold this steady while I break down the sides."

He held out the box as she swiftly collapsed the cardboard around the middle tier. Then she lifted it up and set it carefully on the cake, securing it with metal poles.

She took the smallest box and lifted out the top tier, directing the students to dispose of the cardboard.

The teenagers disappeared, and the two of them

were alone, or as alone as they could be with hundreds of people on the other side of the curtain.

When he got closer, he could see that her hands were shaking. "You okay?"

This time, when she laughed, he could hear the nervousness in it. "Sure."

"The cake looks great. It's everything we talked about."

She didn't respond, instead securing the final tier like she had the middle one. It really was a large cake. But there were a lot of people out there.

"So this will feed eight hundred?" he asked.

"No. I don't expect everyone to eat some. But I have another large, flat cake just in case."

"The way Gertrude and Maude were force-feeding everyone pie, some people might not have room for more sweets."

"I thought so, too. If the extra cake is unused, I'll take it down to the volunteer fire department."

Sandy concentrated while she adjusted a plastic disc underneath the top tier.

"What's that?" Andrew asked.

"It's nothing," she said, too quickly. "I mean, just part of the structure of the cake."

"It turns?"

"Something like that." Her voice had taken on a terse quality, so he didn't press. The crowd beyond the stage clapped again.

"Sounds like the third song's about to start," Sandy said.

"Yes, I better get out there." He turned to the curtain.

"Andrew, wait."

He turned back around. She'd clasped her hands, looking even more nervous than when he first saw her. "You okay?"

"I'm just…" She trailed off, not meeting his eyes. "I'm sorry I didn't go to the centennial meetings. I had a lot going on."

"We managed just fine," he said. His heart sank a little that this was all she wanted to tell him. But he'd take it. At least they were speaking again.

He hesitated, almost asking if it would be all right if he came to see her at the tea shop, but then thought better of it. She had made herself clear. If she felt differently later, she could come to him. This wasn't 1918, like the centennial, and he wouldn't be expected to make all the overtures. She could be the one to come forward next time.

The third song ended. "I'd better go back out," he said.

He slipped back through the curtain and stayed near the microphone as the band played its final number. The walls echoed with the crash of the cymbals, and the blare of the trumpet cut through all other sounds.

The school anthem slid straight into the fight song, and everyone stood to clap along. Andrew felt moved by the tune, one that was so familiar to him, branded in his heart as a student. For just a moment, he wished his father were there to give him advice. How does a man make his way in the world? How does he know when he's found the perfect companion, a wife? How does he go on with life when nothing seems to be working out as planned?

As the fight song wound to a close, Andrew stepped up to the microphone. He flipped it on as the marching band cadenced its way out the door again, leaving the room quiet in its wake.

"Thank you to the band for that amazing rendition of our classic songs and school anthems. Before we move on to a brief history of our town and schools, we will have an undoubtedly brief message from our own Mayor T-bone."

Applause filled the room. For a moment, no one could spot T-bone, who had a newly filled plate of pie and was busily shoveling it into his mouth.

Gertrude strode right up to him, her gray helmet of hair wobbling with indignation, and took the plate out of his hands. She was feeling brave.

She shooed him up to the stage. Those who were close enough to notice their interaction tittered lightly.

T-bone ambled up to the steps. He never looked any different than he did right now, in his motorcycle vest, bare arms, loose jeans with a leather belt and multiple chains.

He was a bit like Santa Claus, as identifiable and never changing.

He clasped the microphone like he was Elvis. "Hel-looooo, citizens of Applebottom!"

Andrew slipped back behind the curtain. "All ready?" he asked Sandy.

The cake was glorious. Sandy stood next to it, holding a piece of paper.

"It's all done," she said. "Andrew, I wondered if I might be the one to describe it."

"Really? You want to talk in front of everyone?" This didn't seem like her at all.

"I'm scared stiff, but I want to."

So that was why she was so well-dressed. "Sure," he said. "It's your cake. If you need me, just signal, and I'll take over."

Sandy turned back to the cake. From the other side of the curtain, T-bone said, "Well, that's it, and goodbye. I'll give this back to Andrew if he ever shows up."

Andrew hurried through the curtain. "Thank you, Mayor," he said. "And now we have the crowning moment of our celebration. You may all know that we have in our midst a renowned cake decorator, Sandy Miller. Her work has been featured in newspapers all over the state, and we are extremely lucky to have one of her incredibly sought-after designs on our very own centennial celebration cake. I've been involved in the process of working on the historical aspects of this cake, and I must say, Sandy has knocked it out of the park."

He turned to the curtain, keeping his mind focused

on his introduction, but still wondering how the town would react to this very public reappearance of the girl they all let down.

Sandy tried to calm her nerves. She could do this. It was just a town. And if she made a complete fool of herself, she could always just leave. Find a job somewhere else. She just had to get through this moment and trust that it would work out.

From the other side of the curtain, she heard Andrew say, "Let's give a round of applause for Sandy and her amazing Applebottom school history cake."

The teen girl on the side of the stage pulled on the ropes to open the curtain.

With the pedestal on its rolling cart, the cake was as tall as Sandy. The audience gasped when they saw it. She knew it was impressive. It was undoubtedly the largest cake she had ever made, and possibly ever would.

She had oiled the wheels on the cart so that as she pushed the cake to the front of the stage it would run smoothly. The last thing she needed was for the cart to snag on a bump and send the cake toppling forward into the crowd.

But it didn't. The cart glided forward until she stopped it next to the microphone.

"Look at that!" Andrew said.

She only cast a side glance at him. He looked ridiculously handsome in his blue sports coat and red tie. Standing next to each other with her in her blue dress, they were the epitome of Applebottom's school pride.

Except, Sandy hadn't been. She had been their biggest outcast.

The whole thing felt so strange and unsettling, and she almost lost her nerve and bolted for the door.

But Andrew stepped away from the mic and locked eyes with her. "Still good?" he asked.

He was giving her an out, somehow sensing her fear. Or maybe it was obvious to everyone. But she steeled herself and walked up to the microphone.

The small stage at the end of the Applebottom high school cafeteria was not large. It was not grand. Moments that changed the world did not happen here. But this moment was possibly about to change her world.

"Andrew and I…" She faltered immediately, realizing she was being too familiar. "Mr. McAllister and I worked for many weeks on the subject matter for this cake. I'm very honored to have been chosen to decorate it."

She turned to the bottom tier.

"Before we cut it, we'll let everyone have a chance to see it up close. But you'll find on this bottom tier, the foundation of Applebottom's community. Forestry. Fishing. And of course, entertainment. We all know that the development of our neighbor Branson as a tourist destination changed the course of history for this part of our state."

She turned the cake on its wheel, revealing the bottom tier as it evolved from pine forest and lakes to construction, docks, and an entire sea of tiny people looking up at a lighted stage meant to depict the performances in Branson that had drawn early crowds.

"The second tier represents Applebottom itself, the town that we know and love so well," she said. The middle revolved smoothly on its disc, showing the shops of Town Square, the park with its gentle hill and lakefront, and of course the elementary, middle, and high schools.

"At the very top of our cake, we have what I hope is the most important part of Applebottom," she said. "Community. This part of the state was built on the arrival of tens of thousands of people from every walk of life, every background, every part of the world."

The top tier showed a collection of tiny people, each one carefully formed so that no two were exactly alike.

"But before I have you come up and look at the cake more closely, I wanted to show off a very special feature of this cake, one that depicts my own spin on cake decorating, which has been a very popular subject of conversation in the last few months. And that's my hidden messages. Secret messages."

She realized that the mostly hushed cafeteria had gone dead silent.

*This was it.*

She twisted the bottom tier until it met its mark, then moved the center one, and finally the top. When they all aligned perfectly, words appeared that flowed from one tier to another, written in the blue of a river that cut through the designs of all parts of the cake.

"The words you see here are acceptance, hope, and love." She cast a furtive glance at Andrew, who was looking at her curiously. Certainly they had never discussed the hidden message in her cake.

"Acceptance is what I am asking for from this community. Not just for me. We all know where I've been. But for everyone here who may have a troubled background, or hit a terrible snag on their way to becoming the person they were meant to be."

She looked out over the crowd, and met the eye of Maude, who was nodding, and the beaming Betty.

"The next word is hope. Hope is what I want for all of us. But particularly for myself. Something amazing got started during the making of this cake, and I feel like I blew it. Just like I blew it eighteen years ago."

Her voice faltered, but she had to finish it.

"The last word is love. I love this town. You did right by my son. But I also love someone in it. One particular person. And even though maybe I shouldn't have put messages to him in all the cakes you all have been eating these last few months, it was all I knew to do."

She tried to make herself look over at Andrew. She could see his sport coat from the corner of her eye. But she couldn't quite do it.

Her voice was about to go. She entire body jangled with nerves at the huge risk she had just taken. She only had one thing left to say.

"My hope is that he will see the message in my cake this time. And he will know that it was for him."

Her voice broke at the end. She stepped away from the microphone and into the shadows. Now she would find out whether that was where she needed to remain, or if this chance she had taken had made a difference.

Andrew stood a little dumbstruck by the cake.

The crowd broke out in applause, then shouts.

"Talk to her!"

"Go get her!"

Andrew stepped up to the microphone, his body turned to her.

"I've been in love with you since I was a teenage boy. I don't think I'm very likely to give it up now."

Sandy's head felt light, as if she were suddenly filled with air.

He had? All those years? Just as she had?

He stepped away from the microphone to find her in the shadows. "I feel like maybe we should get away from the entire town looking at us," he whispered.

"Maybe so," she said.

"That was pretty brave thing you just did."

"It was time to be brave," she said.

The citizens of Applebottom clapped and cheered, and Sadie emerged to organize the line to file by the cake.

Andrew took Sandy's hand and led them deeper backstage.

"The cake…" he said, then trailed off.

"You liked it?" Her throat felt choked off, but she managed to get words out.

"Of course. You are so crazy."

"I am, aren't I?"

"What do we do now?" His eyes moved across her face, as if he were trying to memorize her. She flushed under his attention.

"I thought maybe you would want to come to Caden's game tomorrow. With me."

"There's really no Jerry in the picture?" he asked.

"Jerry? You mean Caden's deadbeat father?"

"You ran out of town to see him. The ladies said he didn't show up again, but…"

"No. He didn't show at the game. And he never called Caden again. Another promise broken. Another threat that turned out to be empty."

"How is Caden taking it?"

"Hard to say. He's an easy-going boy. He's glad he got to meet him, though." Sandy's eyes sparked with emotion that Jerry had gotten anywhere near to her son to disappoint him. She'd really picked wrong back then.

But not today.

"So, the game?" she asked.

"I'd be happy to," he said. "I'm happy to go anywhere you go."

"Even if that means staying in Applebottom?"

"Especially if it means staying in Applebottom."

His hand brushed her hair, and they stood closer together than they'd ever been. Sandy flashed back to that night in front of her house, when she practically ran from him and returned to realize that it had been a mistake, that he might have kissed her if she'd stayed.

Today she would stay.

As they looked at each other, they heard the squeak of the pulleys as the girl pulled the curtain closed.

"I don't think they can see us anymore," Andrew said.

And carefully, tenderly, at the high school where he'd missed his first chance, he kissed her. For one breathless moment, they were teenagers again, their entire futures in front of them.

Only this time, they knew exactly where they were going, and who would be with them on their journey.

# CHAPTER 19

The championship game of the Fisher Junior College Dragons had two minutes left in the fourth quarter.

Andrew held Sandy's hand tightly. He'd become something of a veteran of these games, having traveled with Sandy the entire season. Now it was early December, and the fate of the Dragons rested on the final snap and a trick play that would be nothing short of a miracle for the team to pull off.

"I can't believe they have Caden out there," Sandy said. Her fingers gripped him so tightly that he was beginning to lose feeling in his hand. He worked his way loose and put his arm around her instead.

"The other center isn't having a good game. Caden's the best back up they've got."

"He looks nervous. Don't you think he looks nervous?"

Andrew had no idea what Sandy was seeing in the boy. With his helmet and gear, it was impossible to even recognize his features, much less make out an expression. But he wanted to support her. "I think he's fine. He's going to do just fine."

The teams lined up. Truthfully, the snap wasn't the most essential part of the play. Everyone else had to do their parts. They were going for an onside kick in hopes of getting down the field for one more score to take the win.

Sandy gripped Andrew's waist about as tightly as she had been gripping his hand. They held their breaths as the play clock ticked down.

Caden snapped the ball cleanly to the kicker, and he punted it sideways instead of down the field. Both sides of the stadium jumped to their feet. If the Bulldogs downed the ball as was expected, they could just run the clock out. But if the Dragons were successful in regaining the ball, they could make one last rush for their end zone.

The kick bounced off a Bulldog, making it a live ball. Realizing that the onside kick had worked, both teams piled onto it to get the play down.

The refs ran toward the mound of bodies, pulling players away to determine who had the ball.

Caden wasn't in the fray. As center, he had been too far from the action this time. Andrew looked over at Sandy. She was a definite football mom, leaning forward, her eyes trained on the field. She had a glow about her at a football game that always made him smile.

"Do they have it?" she asked.

Dragon players started jumping up and down, then the cheerleaders, then some of the fans. Finally, the ref made his signal. Turnover. Possession to the Dragons.

Caden turned to the stands and gave his mother a thumbs up. He spotted Andrew and gave a quick nod. He'd been surprised to learn his old history teacher was dating his mom, but the times they'd been together had gone well. Andrew's mother had doted on the boy at Thanksgiving as if he was her own grandson.

Sandy released him and began screaming with her already hoarse voice. "They did it. They did it. They did it!"

Bill leaned past Shannon to say, "And now they have to do something with it."

It was true. They only had forty-five seconds to get the rest of the way down the field. They were down by two. All they needed was a field goal.

The kicking team ran off, and the offense ran on. Caden stayed on the field.

"They're going to have to work fast," Sandy said. The cold made her cheeks and the tip of her nose a rosy pink.

No one had timeouts left, so the players rushed into the new position. They had to make things move. In college, if they got a first down, the clock would stop to move the chains. They had to do at least that much.

Caden snapped the ball, and the quarterback fell back. Now Bill and Shannon leaped to their feet, shouting for their son. The four of them had become couple friends, something unfamiliar to Andrew. But he liked them both, and this friendship mattered a lot to Sandy, who had missed out on all the years of having parent friends while she raised Caden alone outside of town.

"Oh, no, he's risking a pass!" Shannon squealed, barely able to watch through her fingers.

The ball sailed through the air, and at first it seemed there would be no one to receive it. But then out of nowhere, a receiver leapt into the air and brushed it with his fingers, changing his trajectory so that he could grasp it in his arms. He came down hard, but they had gained twenty yards.

The refs stopped the clock to move the chains for the first-down markers.

"That's field goal range," Bill said. "Hot dog, they did it."

"He's still got to make the kick," Shannon said.

Sandy's hand found his and squeezed it to death again. Andrew laughed to himself. If this was the price of getting to attend these games with her, he would pay it.

Fifteen seconds on the clock. The kicking team ran out again.

"How does he look?" Sandy asked.

"Open your eyes and see for yourself."

She did. The teams lined up, and Caden made the snap. The kicker ran forward and everything in the stadium got quiet as the ball sailed toward the goal post.

It bounced on the edge of one of the polls, and then went through.

The response was deafening. The Dragon fans screamed and cried and hugged each other and high-fived and stomped their feet.

Sandy wrapped her arms around Andrew and kissed him full on the mouth.

Andrew held on to the moment. The crisp air. The happy sounds of shouts around him. The announcer counting off the seconds as the clock ran out, and the secondary cheer that went up.

And Sandy, her arms around his neck, her lips on his. Her hair, tickling his cheeks. The warm beautiful weight of her pressing against him.

This was what he had waited for all those years. Small town. Small community. Big life. Big love.

And it was all theirs.

# EPILOGUE

Any minute, Sandy's work would indeed be displayed in the Metropolitan Museum of Art.

This was a big day. One of the biggest. The annual Met Gala.

Sandy stood next to her cake, afraid to move in any direction, lest the bustle of servers and personal assistants and managers and supervisors cause someone to bump into the table.

She had never been this nervous in her life, not even when she'd stood in front of her entire community with a secret message on a cake.

That was nothing compared to this.

A young man in a black shirt and pants pressed his hand to the headset in his ear and strode up to her.

"Cake ready? It's almost time."

Sandy nodded. Her body shook all the way to her shoes.

"The team will escort you in five."

Her phone buzzed. She waited for the man to walk away, then pulled it from the pocket of her all-white baker uniform. She had been given the outfit by the staff and told to wear it precisely as instructed.

A foot-tall white pleated cap stood on her head. The white shirt was long sleeved, and the white pants impeccably cut. Even her shoes were white. Over it all, she had tied a full-length white apron around her neck and behind her waist. She had not been allowed to put anything in the front pockets of the apron, per security rules, so it took a moment to tug the phone from the pants beneath it.

It was Andrew.

*Holding up okay?*

She tapped a quick reply.

*I'm okay. Five minutes until cake. What's it like out there?*

Andrew sent a series of pictures. He had to sneak them, because they definitely weren't allowed. Half of them were partially black because the camera didn't fully come out of his pocket as he snapped blindly.

Sandy had to giggle at the terrible shots. But she did see the face of the famous actor. And even from behind, she recognized all four members of her old favorite teen boy band.

Sandy had to the pinch herself to believe that she was really here. And she had designed the cake everyone would eat.

River Montgomery had made this happen. He'd commissioned a cake so fancy that it had taken her days to complete it. And then it got shipped to New York.

When the director of arts who was coordinating the Gala saw her cake, he immediately hired her. She had spent two weeks in New York meeting with him to plan the cake, and then executing each part of it under the supervision of an assistant art director and their staff.

It had been a stressful experience, but earlier that day, the cake had been photographed by fourteen national magazines plus the Associated Press. Even though her cake would not get nearly as much play as the celebrities and their costumes would, this was going to be a really big deal in all the culinary magazines.

She braced herself for the avalanche of publicity that was sure to come. It had already started. Someone had already whispered that she ought to be flown to England for the upcoming Royal Wedding.

It was a lot to take in.

The man in black returned, this time followed by a magazine model of a woman with upswept blond hair, perfect makeup, and a long white silk gown.

Still, she held a clipboard and had a headset in her ear, meaning that she was really just part of the help, like Sandy. Important help. But still, help.

"Marcella," the man said, "this is Sandy Miller, the cake decorator."

"Nice to meet you." Marcella's eyes scanned the cake.

"Everything looks to be in order." She turned to the man in black. "Where is the pastry chef?"

"He was just here."

A short, elderly man approached, his hands holding his chef hat in place as he hurried. He was also in all white. "I'm here! Sorry. Hat emergency."

Marcella's sharp eyes took him in. "Look left and right," she said.

He turned his head as she asked. "I've got it pinned now."

She nodded. "Looks like we're ready."

Four men dressed exactly like Sandy and the chef, only with shorter hats, approached and took a handle that extended from each corner of the cart.

"We will proceed in order," Marcella instructed. "First, the pastry chef, then the decorator, then the cake." She moved them into position.

Sandy held her breath as they first set the cake into motion, worried as always about it toppling over. Not that this had been left to chance. The cart had been tested, and it glided across the floor as if floating.

Marcella cleared a path as they moved down the hall. "The chef will be introduced, then the decorator, and then the two of you will move aside so that the cake may be presented. You will walk off to stage right, and will stay at the base of the stage. Do not speak. Do not draw attention to yourself."

They had to make sure the help knew that they were *the help*. But it didn't matter. This was an outrageously amazing occasion, and the snooty Marcella wasn't going to wreck it for her, no matter what she said.

They paused outside a set of broad double doors. Marcella pressed her finger to her headpiece and looked away, as if concentrating.

"On my command," she said, as though she were a general and they were about to launch an offensive.

They waited in the corridor. Sandy could just make out the muffled sound of a man talking over the sound system, and the laughter of the crowd. River and Andrew were out there. River had secured invitations, and Sandy had a seat reserved for her.

As soon as the presentation of the cake was over, she would go change and join them. She had missed the meal, but there was still the dance and walking around to spot celebrities.

"In five," Marcella said firmly. "Four, three, two, and go."

A pair of security guards opened the doors from the other side as the chef led the way into the main room.

Sandy felt too overwhelmed to possibly take everything in. The room sparkled. Dresses, jewelry, decorations, twinkling lights. Everywhere were flowers and people and security.

Marcella ushered them to the center of the room. She'd ditched the clipboard somewhere.

The announcer spoke. "And finally, we have our glorious cake depicting this year's theme of tragedy and comedy."

The cloud clapped appreciatively.

"This six-tiered wonder was baked by renowned pastry chef Pierre La Tour. The layers are made of lemon chiffon with almond cream cheese frosting. And we're all going to gain ten pounds just looking at it."

The audience tittered.

"The cake is lavishly decorated to depict the history of dramatic arts by Sandy Miller, the patron decorator of artist River Montgomery."

Really? Patron decorator? Sandy stifled a giggle. She guessed they had to do something to make her seem important.

Marcella gestured at her and Pierre, and they followed her to the corner of the stage. The four cake handlers twirled the cake in a circle so that everyone could see all parts of it.

Sandy looked upon it with pride. Each layer depicted different periods, beginning with the Greek tragedies and going up to Shakespeare, opera and stage plays, silent films and into the modern Hollywood era. A total of seventy-five scenes had been carefully selected by both her and the committee, and hand sculpted to be placed on the cake. It was a momentous work. She would probably never do anything like it again.

The announcer described the more interesting elements of the cake, and then Marcella escorted Sandy and Pierre back into the bowels of the building.

"Thank you for your contribution to this year's

Gala," Marcella said coolly. Her clipboard had mysteriously reappeared.

And with that she was gone.

Sandy hustled to the back storage room where the staff had been instructed to leave their personal belongings. The coat check girl retrieved her garment bag, and Sandy hurried with it to the employee powder room.

It wasn't easy changing into a shimmery evening gown in a bathroom stall, but Sandy was used to making do. The dress itself had been a gift from Andrew's mother, and Sandy treasured it.

Doris McAllister loved Sandy. In the year that Sandy had been dating Andrew, the two of them had formed a close friendship. Doris had become the kind maternal presence that Sandy had never known growing up. Sandy's only aggravation with her was how often she hinted, not so subtly, that her son needed to get his act together and get married.

Why hadn't they? Sandy was happy in her job decorating cakes for Betty, although large bakeries in several major cities had offered her positions. That would get even more intense after tonight. She would be able to move anywhere she wanted.

Not that she did. Andrew had committed to one more year at Applebottom, as none of the college positions he'd considered felt quite right.

But all the opportunities lay before them.

She turned to the mirror, garish and yellow, but at least it was something. Her hair had been elegantly styled into a swirly updo for her earlier that day by the Gala staff. It set off the dark blue dress that shimmered with beads and crystals over the entire bodice and down to the floor.

She tugged at the close fit self-consciously, then turned back to her bag.

Sandy folded up the white baker uniform and apron as well as she could. The outfit was definitely a keepsake.

She returned to the staff check room to hand over the garment bag for safekeeping. The girl looked surprised at Sandy's new outfit. "Are you going in to the ball?"

"I am," Sandy said with a giggle. "I'm River Montgomery's patron decorator."

She cut through the kitchen, where the atmosphere was much more relaxed now that dinner had been served. The process of cutting and serving the cake would take fifteen to twenty minutes, according to the master schedule. She had changed just in time to eat a piece of her own creation.

She tugged her ticket from her purse as she hurried back down the hall to enter the main ballroom as a real person this time.

She was stopped by the guards and showed them her ticket. They called over an usher to escort her to her seat. She was glad for that, because in the sea of tables, she had not managed to spot River or Andrew in the few minutes that she had been inside the room before.

Her nerves settled completely as she slid into the empty chair.

"How was dinner?" she asked.

"Magnificent," River said. "Everyone is talking about your cake."

"And the fact that I'm the patron decorator of artist River Montgomery?" Sandy asked.

River laughed. "And possibly that. No one has ever heard of such a title."

"Well, I am more than honored to be the first."

A waiter leaned near her ear. "Would Madame like a plate or a salad?"

"I'm just here for the cake," she said.

"Coffee?"

"Now that would be amazing," she said.

Andrew leaned in and kissed her cheek. "Did you get to eat?"

"Oh, yes. They had a buffet for the staff. Not exactly what you guys were eating, but it was something."

"Extraordinary, isn't it?" Andrew asked. "I don't feel very small town right now, do you?"

Sandy shook her head. "Definitely not. They're going to want to have a town meeting just to have us talk about it."

Andrew laughed. "They will."

"Isn't that a sad sight to you?" River asked, gesturing to the rapidly disappearing cake.

"It was well-photographed," Sandy said. "I don't have a permanent medium."

"You should. I've heard you're taking a sculpting class."

Sandy grinned at Andrew. "This one bullied me into it. So yes."

"Excellent. I should like a full representation of your work to be sent to my house for temporary exhibits as soon possible."

Sandy's cheeks burned. "I don't think I'm going to be that good."

"Nonsense," River said. "You're a genius. An artist must be full of himself. Otherwise, he will be riddled with self-doubt."

"I'll try to remember that," Sandy said.

The waiter returned with her coffee and a slice of cake.

"All, there it is," River said. "It looks as though you got Marilyn Monroe. How perfect."

"I'm surprised I got one with something on it," Sandy said. "Most of the cake is just going to be random swirls."

Andrew looked down at his piece. It was mostly white. "Obviously the pretty ladies get the best parts."

"As it should be," River said. "It appears that I got half of Romeo's dead body."

Sandy could not control the snorting laugh that came out. "I can't believe they cut it right at his chest."

"It's as if they know me," River said with a dramatic flourish of his fork. "Now, I shall stab his worthy torso." He stuck his fork into the gold fondant tunic.

After the closing remarks, guests were instructed to mingle among the open areas of the museum. River moved on with some of his art friends, and Sandy and Andrew held hands and wandered through the exhibits.

"I've never been to this museum before," Andrew said.

"I've never been to New York before. These two weeks were a whirlwind. I can't wait to do some actual sightseeing."

Andrew stopped them in front of a glorious portrait of a woman and her child in the middle of one of the smaller halls. He gazed at the image of the woman cradling her infant. They were both dressed in simple peasant clothing with rough fabrics, but their cheeks were rosy, and happiness emanated from both their faces.

Sandy couldn't take her eyes off of Andrew. In his black tuxedo, he looked even more handsome than in his sport coats. Together the two of them looked downright big city. She had certainly never pictured a moment like this ever happening to her. Not in all those years that she struggled with an angry mother and a little boy.

"Can you believe we're here?" she asked.

He turned to her. "Absolutely. You were always destined to have your work in front of important people."

She laughed. "I guess I did manage to get my work in

the Metropolitan Museum of Art. Even if it did end up in everyone's stomach."

He drew her close. "It's the beginning of wonderful things."

"It's already wonderful."

They walked on, leaving the back side of the exhibit, and into the great hall, filled with people and chatter. They passed the fountains and moved into a garden, which was quieter since the air had turned cool, even for May.

A photographer approached. "May I take your picture?" he asked.

Andrew's grip on her fingers tightened. "Actually, I would love that. Especially if you would stay just a moment."

The man nodded and lifted his camera to his face.

"Step up here," Andrew said, guiding her to stand on the wide marble ledge about a foot off the ground, just in front of a fountain.

"Oh, I'm not exactly important," Sandy said, her face growing warm. "I only decorated the cake."

"I got to photograph that," the man said. "It was splendid!"

"Thank you."

Andrew was waiting patiently for her to step up, so she lifted the hem of her long dress and rose above him.

"That's lovely—" the photographer said, then cut off abruptly when Andrew got down on one knee, holding out a black velvet box. "Oh!" He began firing flashes at them.

"Andrew?" What was he doing? Her hands pressed to her cheeks.

Andrew gazed up at her, his expression earnest. "Sandy, almost twenty years ago I waited too long and missed my chance to make you mine. I'm not going to make that mistake again."

He lifted the lid. Inside, a simple square-cut diamond rested on a velvet cushion. It sparkled in the twinkling light above their heads.

"I've loved you since I was too young to know what the word meant. But I know it now. And I would be so honored if you would allow me to love you for the rest of my life. Will you marry me?"

A small crowd had gathered around them, realizing a proposal was happening. Everybody loves love.

But Sandy kept her focus on Andrew. His eyes held hers, anxious for her answer. He already felt like home to her. This would only make it official.

A few of the other photographers caught on to the moment, and more flashes bounced off the crystal beads of her gown.

"Yes!" she said. "Of course. Of course I will."

A great cheer went up from the crowd, and the applause made her smile. She held out her hand and Andrew slipped the ring on her finger. She lifted him to stand on the ledge with her, for what was taking a risk in front of famous strangers unless you did it together?

The flashes continued to fire as Andrew turned her to face him. Sandy remembered that first night he might have kissed her, after visiting River. And the first time he actually did, behind the curtain at the Applebottom centennial when she confessed how she felt about him.

Now he had shown his feelings to her.

Their lips met, warm and familiar. There had been many kisses in between, but this one topped them all. It was the kiss of promise, of commitment, the kiss of forever.

Her love for Andrew clicked into place, as easy and wondrous as the one she felt for her child, both strong and true.

They'd emerged from their pasts, a little jostled and a little bruised. But free nonetheless. The only thing they needed now was to enjoy the future that waited for them.

This was a good start.

*Yay for Sandy!*

I hope you still nurture your dreams no matter what life has thrown at you.

Don't miss the wedding of Sandy and Andrew, as witnessed by hard-talking, curmudgeonly Gertrude! Fans who receive text or email messages from Abby receive an exclusive bonus epilogue for every book!

Sign up to get it on her web site!

If you loved the advice football coach Carter McBride gave Andrew, read all about the romance between Carter and Ginny (as well as her crazy untrained Great Dane) in *The Perfect Disaster*.

# GERTRUDE & MAUDE'S CHOCOLATE REFRIGERATOR PIE

(Good for fattening up anybody.)

CRUST

- **1 1/2 cups finely crushed chocolate cookie crumbs** (Gertrude eats the centers out of the Oreos and uses the leftover tops and bottoms. )
(*Maude, leave me out of these instructions. You know good and well the white centers of an Oreo are the best part, otherwise why would they make double stuff?*)
(Fine, Gertrude. But you should mention that Golden Oreos work just as well, or you can crush a sleeve of graham crackers.)
(*I will do no such thing. It's chocolate Oreos or else it isn't our pie!*)

(Well, at least tell them how many Oreos it takes to make a crust.)

(*How should I know? I eat too many of them to count. More than a row and less than a package.*)

**• 6 tablespoons melted unsalted butter**

(You can use salted butter, but your crust will end up tasting as salty as Gertrude's attitude. )

FILLING

**• 1/4 cup hot water**

**• 1 1/2 tablespoons cocoa**

(*Maude makes us buy the fancy Ghirardelli kind but any kind will do. Don't be fancy like Maude.*)

**• 2 teaspoons vanilla**

(*We order Mexican vanilla but any extract will do. That's Maude getting fancy again.*)

**• 1 cup semi-sweet chocolate chips**

(No, Gertrude, bittersweet, not semi-sweet.)

(*No, Maude, it's semi-sweet. I buy the ingredients. Bittersweet is like dark chocolate and the pie will be too tart.*)

(All right, Gertrude, but don't blame me when your teeth fall out.)

• **1 cup heavy cream**

• **2 teaspoons granulated sugar**

• **1/8 teaspoon salt**

INSTRUCTIONS

1. Preheat the oven to 375°F. Lightly grease a 9-inch pie pan.
2. For the crust: Mix up the crumbs and melted butter, and press the mixture into the bottom and up the sides of the pan. Freeze the crust for 20 minutes, then bake for 8 minutes. It should be browned around the edges. Allow to cool. (Gertrude, remember that time you forgot to freeze it and it burnt to a crisp? *Don't bring that up now, Maude.* But you tried serving it to Alfred Felmont, and you didn't know it was burnt because it was already so dark brown, and he was all polite and ate the whole thing? *He's a gentleman, Maude.* And then you ate it later and spit it out in the sink? *That's enough, Maude. These people are trying to make a pie.*)
3. For the filling: Mix the hot water, cocoa, and vanilla in a small bowl and set aside.
4. Heat the chocolate in a saucepan on low heat.

Stir until completely melted, and allow it to cool for five minutes.

5. Whip the cream, sugar, and salt with a mixer until it forms soft peaks.

6. Stir the cocoa mixture into the melted chocolate.

7. Whisk the chocolate mixture into the whipped cream until the color is uniform.

8. Spread the filling into the cooled crust.

9. Refrigerate the pie until the filling is firm. Don't panic if it jiggles for a while. (*Like Maude jiggles when she gets in a hurry.* Now, Gertrude. Your arm wings flap like a bird when you're excited. *Oh, be quiet.*)

**Enjoy your pie and don't miss more of Gertrude and Maude in the next Applebottom book:**
***The Perfect Disaster* !**

Abby Tyler loves puppy dogs, pie, and small towns (she grew up in one!) Her Applebottom Matchmaker Society books combine the sweet and wholesome style of romance she loves with the funny, sometimes a-little-too-truthful characters she remembers from growing up in a place where everyone knew everybody's business.

Join her mail or text list for a bonus epilogue for every book, a wedding scene narrated by Gertrude!

The Applebottom Matchmaker Society books include:

- *The Sweetest Match*

- *The Perfect Disaster*
- *The Irresistible Spark*

*with many more planned!*

facebook.com/authorabbytyler

twitter.com/abbytylerauthor

instagram.com/abbytylerauthor

www.ingramcontent.com/pod-product-compliance
Lightning Source LLC
Chambersburg PA
CBHW030628190726
48286CB00008B/2438